'Whatever's th...
Have you had s...

'In a way,' he repli... I've been left half a million pounds.'

'Wow!' said Claire. 'That's the kind of bad news I like!'

'There's more to it,' he said solemnly. 'Much more. It was from a man, an American. I'd never heard of this man, George Merrick, until my mother told me last night that he's left me all this money. He's also left her a considerable sum.'

'That's very odd,' said Claire. 'You'd think at least you'd have heard his name mentioned before, wouldn't you?'

'Precisely. Who was this man? I asked her. At first she was coy about it, saying he was someone who'd been in the construction industry like my father.' He paused and gave a hollow laugh. 'Or should I say the man I'd always believed was my father!'

'Oh,' said Claire quietly.

'Then I got the truth from her: she had a brief affair with this George Merrick and became pregnant. I'm thirty-two years old and have only just discovered who my real father is!'

Barbara Hart was born in Lancashire and educated at a convent in Wales. At twenty-one she moved to New York, where she worked as an advertising copywriter. After two years in the USA she returned to England to become a television press officer in charge of publicising a top soap opera and a leading current affairs programme. She gave up her job to write novels. She lives in Cheshire and is married to a solicitor. They have two grown-up sons.

Recent titles by the same author:

THE EMERGENCY SPECIALIST
THE DOCTOR'S LOVE-CHILD
ENGAGING DR DRISCOLL

THE GPs' WEDDING

BY
BARBARA HART

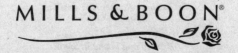

MILLS & BOON®

For Irene

First published in Great Britain 2003
Harlequin Mills & Boon Limited,
Eton House, 18-24 Paradise Road, Richmond, Surrey TW9 1SR

© Barbara Hart 2003

ISBN 0 263 83452 2

Set in Times Roman 10½ on 12 pt.
03-0603-46955

Printed and bound in Spain
by Litografia Rosés, S.A., Barcelona

CHAPTER ONE

DR CLARE WESTWOOD was settling in to her new job at The Hawthorns medical centre in Kelsale with ease as well as enthusiasm.

Her enthusiasm for new ventures could usually be taken for granted. It was part of her nature, inherited from her Irish mother along with her flame-red hair. The ease she felt was partly due to the warm welcome she'd received from the other three doctors—Fabian, Sam and Brian—but most of all because the medical centre was attached to a large general hospital, St Margaret's, known to all as Maggie's.

'Isn't that a brilliant idea? A hospital right on the doorstep!' she'd said to her boyfriend, Jason, who'd first alerted her to the job vacancy after Fabian had spoken to him about it. Fabian Drumm was a very good friend of Jason's—he'd known him since their medical student days, but whereas Fabian had completed medical school and went on to qualify as a GP, Jason had dropped out after failing his final exams and had gone to work for a pharmaceutical company.

'Fabian says it's an experimental idea,' said Jason. 'The Hawthorns is one of the first GP practices in the country to be set up in this way, attached to a hospital. But I'm sure Fabian will tell you all about it himself when you meet him at the interview.'

Clare was anxious that such a desirable-sounding position might attract dozens of applications, but she needn't have worried. Fabian, Sam and Brian were unanimous in offering her the job.

Her surgery was next to Fabian's and on her first day he walked in with two cups of coffee. He paused for a moment, taking in his new partner's striking looks—distractingly pretty face and the shoulder-length red hair—before handing a cup to her. She was looking remarkably relaxed for a newcomer…but even at the interview, he recalled, she'd shown few nerves.

'I don't know how you like it,' he said, 'but will this do?'

She looked around her freshly decorated room with its modern furniture and fittings. 'It's fabulous,' she replied. 'It's like working in a Scandinavian furniture store…all this Norwegian wood and gleaming polished steel.'

'I meant the coffee, actually,' said Fabian solemnly. 'It's got milk but no sugar—and it's not decaffeinated.'

'Ah, yes!' she said brightly. 'That's just how I like it. If you've a moment to spare why not drink your coffee here?'

'Sure,' he said, finding himself a chair. 'That's what I had in mind.'

Clare waited for Fabian to say something to start off the conversation, but when she realised that this handsome, serious-faced man was content to remain silent during his coffee-break, Clare felt the urge to chat. It was one of her shortcomings, she acknowledged, that she needed to fill any unnaturally long gaps in conversation with words of her own. At her parents' house the whole place buzzed with noise of one kind or another, usually gossipy chit-chat between her mother and her friends, or music or animated argument—sometimes good-natured, sometimes vehement and opinionated, but always interesting. And the apartment she shared with Jason, her boyfriend of almost one year, was usually just as lively, with friends and relatives constantly calling round or phoning up. Jason himself was a man who rarely stopped talking. That was probably why he was such a good salesman. 'He's got the gift of the gab, all right,' commented her mother approvingly.

'Any woman in your life?' Clare ventured after she'd taken a couple of sips of her coffee.

Dr Fabian Drumm blinked as if a spotlight had been shone into his eyes, surprised at the directness of her first question.

'Er, no,' he said. Then, feeling he'd been put on the spot by his new medical partner, added, 'Too busy for that kind of thing, I'm afraid.'

Clare smiled warmly at him. He really was a bit of a dish...the dark, brooding type.

'I find that hard to believe,' she said wickedly. 'Jason tells me you were quite a ladies' man in medical school.'

Fabian grinned back at her. The smile lit up his face. 'I think your boyfriend is confusing me with himself.'

'That figures!' Clare replied.

'He's doing well, I hear, in the pharmaceutical business. He keeps reminding me how much more he's earning now than if he'd ended up a humble doctor.'

'You must come round for a meal one evening,' said Clare. 'I've heard so much about you from Jason that I feel I know you as a friend already.'

'I'd love to,' he replied. 'But from the sound of what Jason's been telling you, I think I'm going to have to put the record straight. He's good at make-believe, is

our friend Jason. But I'm sure you've found that out
for yourself!'

'Indeed I have! But then I come from a family where
that's the norm. My mother's one of six children and
each one can tell a different story about the same event.
But we're Irish so a bit of the blarney is allowed, ex-
pected even. Jason has no excuse at all. I bet he told
you that we met in a pub, didn't he?'

'Yes, I think he did.'

'Well, we didn't! We met when he came to promote
his company's products at the GP practice where I used
to work. He thinks it sounds sexier saying we met in
a pub.'

Fabian laughed, a deep rich chuckle. 'That sounds
like Jason—making up stories even when he doesn't
need to! It's a pity he didn't use the same ingenuity
when taking his medical exams. He'd have passed with
flying colours.'

'Oh, I think he's happier the way he is now,' said
Clare. 'He likes the money—whereas we prefer the job
satisfaction, you and I.' She hesitated for a moment
before adding, 'Or am I making assumptions?'

'No, you're not making assumptions. I love the
work. A little more money would be nice, but I'm
happy doing what I've always wanted to do…being a
doctor.' Fabian drained his cup and got up to leave.
'Back to the grindstone,' he said.

Clare's eyes followed him as he walked out of her
room, his tall athletic body moving with the grace of
a panther. He is certainly an attractive proposition is
our Dr Drumm, thought Clare in a purely detached,
objective way.

'Tell me more about your friend Fabian,' said Clare
when she and Jason had settled down to their evening

meal—a chicken stir-fry with rice and Chinese vegetables, one of Jason's favourites.

'You're suddenly very interested in him,' her boyfriend replied teasingly. 'Finding him sexy, are you?'

'He's my work colleague. Of course I'm interested in him, but not in that way! I'm also interested in Brian and Sam, but as you don't happen to know them it's no use asking you for the low-down. I'll have to do some discreet enquiring from the practice nurse or the receptionist about the other two doctors. But Fabian, now *he's* a bit of a mystery man, I think. After all, you told me he was very successful with women at college. That's what you said…' She was going to add 'but he denied it', then thought the better of it. She didn't want Jason to think she'd been discussing Fabian's sex life with the man himself.

'He was very popular with women,' confirmed Jason, 'but I think that was because he always appeared so brooding and cool… It turned him into a kind of enigma and a challenge. The female medical students were just lining up to throw themselves at his feet!'

'Is that so?' replied Clare. 'Well, he won't find me scratching at his door. I like a man to be more straightforward. I can't be doing with all this moody, mysterious stuff. I like a man who speaks his mind, calls a spade a spade, states what he wants—'

'In that case,' interrupted Jason, 'I'll have some more stir-fry.'

Later that evening, when they were watching a French film with subtitles on TV, Jason suddenly said, 'He's French, you know. Well, half-French anyway.'

'Who is?' asked Clare distractedly. 'They're *all* French, aren't they? It's a French film!'

'Fabian,' replied Jason. 'His mother is French and his father English. I think he must take after her in his personality. All dark and brooding and Gallic. Women find that irresistible.'

Clare shifted uneasily in her chair. 'Not this woman.'

All the patients were new to Clare, but during her first week she'd seen one particular woman three times.

Gail Thewlis was a thin, nervous, colourless woman who presented with a series of unrelated symptoms on each occasion. These ranged from a sore throat to a pain in the ankle and stomach cramps. After giving the woman a thorough examination each time, Clare couldn't find anything particularly wrong with her. She had her suspicions that Gail's problems were purely in her mind—or possibly that she was going through an early menopause and the drop in her hormone levels was causing her to be anxious. She was certainly very highly strung on the three occasions she'd walked into Clare's surgery.

'I can't find anything to worry about, Mrs Thewlis,' she told the sad-faced woman on her third visit, 'but just to make absolutely certain I think a blood test would be a good idea. Perhaps you're a little anaemic.' Clare wrote out the blood-test request form and handed it to her. 'St Margaret's path lab will fit you in without an appointment, so you can go there straight away. It's handy being so close, isn't it?'

Clare smiled encouragingly but Gail Thewlis didn't move from her seat or even reach out a hand to take the form. Instead she broke down in tears, gripping her head in her bony hands.

Clare got up and went round to comfort the woman. 'Is there anything else bothering you?' she asked.

'It's *him*,' said Gail between sobs. 'My husband. He's gone funny in the head. I don't know what to do!'

'Tell me about it,' said Clare gently. 'Is your husband one of our patients?'

Gail nodded. 'Dr Drumm's. But he won't come to the surgery to see him. He said he'd murder me if I tried to make him.'

'Seriously?' Clare asked with concern. 'He's threatened to murder you?'

'I don't think he means it, but he says things like that all the time. Ever since he lost his job. He was fired because he punched his boss on the nose.' Gail wiped her face with the flat of her hand. 'I was proud of him at the time.'

'What happened?' Clare returned to her chair now that Gail seemed to be calming down and prepared to give the real story behind her problems.

'His boss was a bully, that's what Steve said.'

'Steve's your husband?'

Gail nodded in confirmation. 'He kept telling me stories about this boss and how he was treating Steve like a slave…and how he'd been saying awful things about me…that he going to…to have sex with me given half the chance. Except he didn't use those words.'

'Good heavens!' said Clare. 'I'm not surprised Steve punched him.'

'That's what I thought. But I'm now beginning to wonder if it was all in Steve's mind. All made up. Because he acts so strangely, saying and doing the weirdest things.'

'Can you persuade your husband to make an appointment with Dr Drumm?' Clare asked. 'That would be the best thing.'

'He won't come. He says there's nothing wrong with

him. It's other people that are the problem, he says.
Everyone else is mad, even me. That's what he says.'
Gail sat clasping and unclasping her hands.

'Has he ever used physical violence on you?' Clare
enquired, wondering whether this was a case that
should be reported to the police.

'No,' Gail admitted. 'He's all talk, really. Like I said,
it's all in his head. He just needs help.'

'Then try and persuade him to come and see us,'
said Clare. 'And it's still a good idea for you to have
the blood test. Come and see me in a few days' time
when we have the results—and perhaps we need to
prescribe a mild tranquilliser to help you cope in the
immediate future.'

When Gail Thewlis had left, Clare made a note in
her file—and another note about Steve Thewlis that she
intended to give to Fabian. At the end of morning surgery she placed it in his in-tray and went out for a bite
of lunch.

There was a wonderful, unspoilt pub close to The
Hawthorns called the Builders' Arms. It was a favourite haunt of the doctors from the medical centre. Many
of the hospital staff found their way in there at lunchtime too—although their own hospital canteen was
very popular because its prices were so cheap.

Clare knew that if Fabian, Sam and Brian were
around at lunchtime they could usually be found at
their regular table near the snug bar. Today it was just
Fabian and Brian who greeted her when she joined
them. She squeezed in next to Fabian. 'I've left a note
for you,' she told him. 'It's about one of your patients.'

'Hey,' scolded Brian, 'remember the rules. No work
talk in the pub. We need a complete break to preserve
our sanity.'

'Oops, sorry,' said Clare. 'You never told me that rule before. I know the one about no alcohol at lunch-time if we're seeing patients. Are there any other rules I should know about? Is there one about clean under-wear every month whether we need it or not?' She grinned teasingly at the older man.

Fabian went to the bar and ordered their food—home-made soup and freshly cut sandwiches. He car-ried three soft drinks back to their table.

'At my previous practice we used to allow ourselves a half pint of beer or lager,' said Clare, picking up her soda water and lime juice. 'You must all be saints at The Hawthorns to be so strong-willed.'

A quick glance passed between Fabian and Brian, their expressions revealing nothing. After a short si-lence Brian spoke.

'Actually, it's all my fault,' said Brian, colouring up.

Fabian jumped in. 'Brian, it's not. We all happen to think it's not a good idea to breathe alcohol fumes all over our patients.'

'You might as well tell her,' said Brian, gazing into his half-drunk cola.

'Tell me what?' said Clare, bemused. 'Were you all a load of drunks or something?' She laughed brightly.

'That's not so far from the truth,' said Brian quietly. 'I'm an alcoholic.'

'Oh, dear,' said Clare. 'I'm sorry, I didn't mean to—'

'You're a *former* alcoholic,' said Fabian. 'It was a long time ago and it's all over. You're fine.'

'There's no such thing as a former alcoholic,' said Brian. 'At AA anyone will tell you that. We're just alcoholics who don't drink. That's what I am and that's what I intend to stay.' He turned to Clare. 'I had a lucky escape. I didn't do any harm to my patients through my drinking and my partners have been very supportive. I'm not going to let them down.'

Clare reached out and touched Brian on the hand. 'That's great, Brian,' she said with feeling. 'Did you get support at home as well? From a wife, or anything?'

Their sandwiches arrived and Brian said nothing until the waitress had put all the plates down on the table. Then he said, 'No wife. She left me and that's why I started drinking in the first place. But I've got a terrific girlfriend, Catrina. She's a ''super-nurse''. That's her job description not my biased opinion.'

'A super-nurse? I've not heard of one of those,' replied Clare. 'Does she work at Maggie's?'

'Yes. It's one of the first hospitals in the country to be implementing the scheme. She started off as a ordinary nurse at St Margaret's and then applied to become one of these new nurse consultants. It means that the health service won't be losing skilled nurses from the wards because they can progress within clinical nursing rather than having to go into management to get promotion.'

'What extra things can they do?'

'They can carry out minor operations,' explained Brian, 'and do diagnostic procedures. The kind of things that previously would have been done by a doctor.'

'Taking the bread out of our mouths, then!' joked Clare. 'Seriously, Brian, it sounds a very good idea and I'm all for it. I'd like to meet her some time.' Then, realising that she appeared to have been cutting Fabian out of the conversation, she said, 'How's your sandwich? Mine's delicious.'

'Pretty good,' replied Fabian.

'It comes up to your high French standards?' she asked mischievously.

'How did you know I was French...well, half-French? Ah, don't tell me. Jason? He was always obsessed about it. He was convinced he could detect a French accent even though it's years since I lived in France.'

'Now you come to mention it, there is just the slightest hint. But hardly Maurice Chevalier or 'Allo 'Allo.' Clare winked at him and she found herself gazing into his meltingly soft brown eyes. For a moment she was speechless. 'It's very attractive,' she said, her voice becoming husky.

Fabian looked away. Was she flirting with him? He found it hard to work out just when Clare Westwood was serious and when she was joking. She was, after all, the girl of one of his best friends and therefore off-limits.

'Don't you start,' he said, frowning. 'I had enough trouble with Jason constantly ordering frogs-legs sandwiches and snails on toast for me whenever we went anywhere that served food.'

'Did you grow up in France?' she asked.

'Yes. My father's English but he worked for a large multinational construction company and was based for many years in their Paris office. I went to school in France but went to medical school over here because by that time my parents had divorced and my father was back living in England.'

'I'm sorry,' said Clare, 'about the divorce.'

'It made very little difference to me,' said Fabian. 'My father had ignored my mother and me for as long as I can remember. There were no terrible scenes. The only benefit I derived from having a father was the dual nationality he bestowed on me. I found that quite useful.' He drained his glass. 'More fizzy drinks, anyone?'

By late afternoon, when Clare had returned from her house calls, she saw that there were quite a few patients waiting to see the doctors.

The moment she walked into her surgery there was an uproar outside and one of the patients who had been in the waiting area burst into her room.

'What's she been saying?' shouted the man, his eyes wild. 'What's that cow of a wife been saying about me?'

Clare was startled and more than a little scared that the man might attack her.

'Who are you?' she said, keeping her voice calm.

'Steve Thewlis, that's who. My wife came in here this morning, she said, and told you all about me! Well, she'd no bloody right to do that! You're not my doctor and you and her have no right to talk about me!'

He thumped the desk, sending paperwork leaping into the air.

'Oh!' Clare cried out involuntarily in reaction. At that same moment Fabian came rushing in.

'Are you all right?' he asked her, trying to take in the situation. 'Have you been threatened?'

Clare shook her head. 'I don't think so. This man is the husband of one of my patients, Gail Thewlis. He seems to have some sort of grievance or complaint. Isn't that so, Mr Thewlis?'

Fabian looked questioningly at the man who had been the cause of the commotion. Steve Thewlis was now standing calmly and meekly as if nothing had happened, an air of innocence on his face.

'Steven Thewlis?' Fabian asked.

'That's me,' replied the man.

'You're one of my patients, aren't you? If you take a seat in the waiting area I'll see you in a few minutes,' Fabian said in an attempt to take the heat out of the situation. He moved towards the door expecting Thewlis to follow him. But he didn't. Instead the man started banging on Clare's desk again.

'I am *not* going to see you, Dr Drumm!' Thewlis shouted, his calmer mood now replaced by his earlier angry one.

Fabian continued walking the few paces to the open door. He then closed it firmly and walked back to face the patient.

'Just calm down, Mr Thewlis,' Fabian said, his voice low but firm. 'Sit down and tell us what your problem is.'

'*I'm* not the one with the problem!' Thewlis said, raising his voice. 'It's her!' He pointed an accusing finger at Clare. 'She's been trying to get me to come in and see her. Putting pressure on me. Getting my wife to put pressure on me.'

'Dr Westwood was just concerned about you, that's all,' Fabian said, remembering the note that Clare had left for him about this particular patient. 'I believe she suggested that you make an appointment to see me as I'm your doctor.' Fabian put a hand on Steve's arm in an attempt to get him to move towards the door. 'Just wait outside and I'll make sure I see you—'

Thewlis leapt away from Fabian's touch. 'I am *not* seeing you!' Thewlis said with vehemence. 'You're having an affair with my wife! You are the last person I want to talk to.'

Clare's mouth fell open. 'That's a terrible accusation,' she spluttered. 'Retract it at once!'

Fabian, however, ignored Steve's remark and asked him gently, 'Are you on any medication? I checked your file a few minutes ago, as a matter of fact, but there's nothing on it to indicate that we've prescribed any drugs for you.'

'Drugs? Now he's accusing me of being a drug addict!' Thewlis addressed this last remark to Clare, cutting Fabian out of the conversation. 'He'll be asking me for a blood sample next so he can falsify the result and hand me over to the police! With me safely put away in nick that would leave the field wide open for him to carry on with my wife! I know his game... I know what he's up to!'

'If you don't want to see Dr Drumm then I'd be happy to see you, Mr Thewlis,' Clare said, doing her best to pacify him. 'But first of all you have to calm down and then I can try to help you.'

'I don't need help from anyone!' he shouted. 'I just want to be left alone.' He put his hands up to his head, pressing the palms against his temples.

'Do you have a headache, Mr Thewlis?' Fabian asked.

'Of course I have a bloody headache and it's all your fault! All this pressure is doing my head in.'

'We can help you,' Fabian said coaxingly. 'We can arrange to do investigations to find out why you're having these headaches and mood swings.'

'Mood swings? Who said anything about mood swings?' Thewlis turned to Clare, again cutting out Fabian. 'He just wants to get me sectioned...have me locked up in a lunatic asylum in case he can't make the drugs charge stick. Well, you can tell him I'm not seeing anybody! And you can also tell him to keep his hands off my wife!'

He stormed out of the room, slamming the door behind him. Fabian went after him, leaving Clare alone in the room in a state of mild shock. She'd had difficult patients before and it always left her feeling drained. She slumped into her chair.

A few moments later, Fabian returned and came over to her.

'Thewlis moved so fast he'd gone before I could catch up with him,' he said. 'But I don't suppose it would have done much good even if I had. He was determined not to seek medical advice.'

He crouched next to Clare's chair and put a comforting arm around her.

'Are you all right?'

'I guess so,' she replied. 'But what are we going to do about him? He needs help before he does something dangerous to himself or someone else. What do you think is the cause of his erratic behaviour? Has he acted like this before?'

Fabian shook his head. 'No. I don't think I've set eyes on him more than a couple of times since I've been at The Hawthorns. When I got your note I checked his file…but it shows very little, just the occasional antibiotic and that's about it. I'd say that on the surface of it Steve Thewlis appeared to be a very healthy man. Until now.'

'I really wish he'd stayed for an examination,' said Clare. 'My initial thoughts were that he might have a brain tumour, particularly with the headaches and mood swings.'

'My thoughts entirely,' Fabian said. 'But he was also displaying classic symptoms of mental illness—and until we get to do even a preliminary examination we won't know in which direction we should be going for treatment.'

'I'm worried about him,' said Clare. 'I'm worried that he could be a danger to others in his present mood. What do you think we should do?'

Fabian shrugged. 'There's not a lot we can do until...' He was about to say 'until he hurts someone, or himself' but he left the words unsaid.

He put a hand on Clare's shoulder. 'My instincts tell me I should alert the police,' said Fabian, 'but it's a difficult case. There's nothing in his history to suggest violence or mental illness—and then there's patient confidentiality. We can't just phone up the cops purely because a patient accuses me of having an affair with his wife.' He gave her a friendly squeeze. 'I'm not, by the way. Having an affair with Mrs Thewlis.'

Clare laughed at the absurdity of the accusation. 'After meeting Gail Thewlis I can safely say that I believe you without the merest shadow of a doubt.' She chuckled. 'If you're going to risk getting struck off the medical register I would imagine you'd go for someone a little more...' She shrugged as she cast around for the right words to describe Fabian's perfect woman.

He stroked her hair; its lustrous, fiery tresses had fascinated him from the moment he'd first seen her. 'Someone like you, do you mean?'

He didn't know why he'd said it. The words had come unbidden and he regretted saying them instantly. He rose to his feet and carried on talking before she could respond.

'About Steve Thewlis,' he said, 'we can't just do nothing. I think I'll call and see him tomorrow on my rounds.'

Clare was hesitant. 'I don't think you should go on your own. After all, if you just turn up it will convince him all the more that you're having an affair with his missus. I'd better come with you. You also need a witness in case he starts making more false accusations.'

Fabian smiled briefly. 'Good idea. I'll just go back to my room and make a note of what happened today. We may be needing evidence of threats if we're eventually going to have to section him. That would be the best outcome for all concerned…get him into St Margaret's psychiatric unit so that he can be monitored for seventy-two hours.'

As he was leaving her room, Clare called after him, 'About that meal, can you come this Friday?'

Fabian paused for a minute, checking his personal diary. 'That would be fine, thanks. I'll look forward to it.'

'Seven-thirty, is that OK?' said Clare. 'Do you know where we live? You haven't been to the apartment before, have you?'

'Yes, yes and no,' said Fabian. 'Seven-thirty is OK, and I do know where you live. I've got the address and I can find it in the *A to Z*. And, no, I haven't been before. Jason and I tend to meet in town, which is halfway between both our homes. That was the excuse he always gave me, anyway. I now suspect it was because he didn't want me meeting his gorgeous girlfriend.'

Clare felt herself blushing at this unexpected compliment. 'How far away do you live?' she asked. She and Jason lived six miles from the medical centre.

'Ten miles,' he replied, 'in the opposite direction.'

'In that case, why don't you bring your toothbrush and stay the night? Otherwise it's going to be quite a long drive back for you…and staying over means you can indulge in a glass or two of booze, unlike at lunch-time.'

Fabian pondered the very sensible suggestion. 'Well, as long as it's no bother…it would certainly be more relaxing.'

As he left the room, Clare sighed and continued looking dreamily at the door even when he'd disap-peared from sight, conjuring up the image of her new medical partner. The more she got to know him, the more she liked him. *Really* liked him. She was begin-ning to change her mind about dark, brooding Gallic types. Perhaps they did have a lot going for them, after all.

As arranged, Clare and Fabian called in on Gail and Steve Thewlis the following day. But as it turned out it was a waste of time.

There was no reply after they'd rung the doorbell several times. It was hard to tell whether the Thewlises were out or whether they'd just decided not to answer.

'Should we ask their neighbours if they've seen them, do you think?' Clare asked.

Fabian looked along the street of shabby houses and shook his head. 'It will start to look as if we're ha-rassing them if we do that. Let's try again in a few days' time. Or perhaps you could telephone Gail in a day or so to check she's OK?'

'She'll be coming in to see me in three or four days for the results of her blood test,' Clare said.

They walked back to Fabian's car—a sleek, black, sports model that was his pride and joy. 'I don't want to return to the days when any aberrant behaviour could mean being locked away in a lunatic asylum but we seem to have gone to the other extreme now…when we have to wait until something dreadful happens before an uncooperative patient can be checked out for mental instability and given treatment.'

'Vote for Dr Drumm and the good old days of Bedlam!' said Clare as she stepped into the car. 'That was a joke, by the way. In very bad taste, but then that's me for you!'

He switched on the engine and grinned without looking at her. She was a ray of sunshine with her quick wit and bright outlook on life. No wonder Jason was madly in love with her.

'Jason, have you opened the red wine to let it breathe?' Clare called through from the kitchen.

'Yes, of course I have,' replied her boyfriend, cradling his second glass of chilled white wine.

'Anything we can do to help?' offered Fabian who was also on his second pre-dinner drink.

'Oh, leave her,' said Jason. 'She loves doing the domestic thing. All these career girls are the same. They want the world to know that they can have it all. Perfect job, perfect home, perfect children…all that kind of thing.'

Fabian looked enquiringly at Jason. 'So you're planning on…?'

'No, no…not children,' said Jason quickly. 'Not yet anyway.' He turned to check they were alone and, lowering his voice, said, 'And maybe not with Clare.' He eyed Fabian and put his finger to his lips.

'What do you mean?'

Jason, speaking almost in a whisper, leaned closer to him so that their faces were almost touching. 'I need to talk to you about something. In private. Let's meet in town one evening. Don't say anything to Clare.'

The first thought that entered Fabian's head was that Clare was unable to have children and Jason possibly wanted to discuss their fertility problems with him. Before he could dwell too long on this, Clare shouted cheerily from the kitchen, 'I wouldn't mind another glass of wine, you two. This cook, even though wonderfully in control, gets very thirsty.'

Clare had prepared a wonderful meal. Three courses, each perfectly presented.

'I've got loads of cookbooks,' she said, 'but I can only make a meal if there's a picture of it. It's no good giving me something just written down—I need to see it in full glorious colour before I can even start.'

'This is delicious,' said Fabian, eating the scallops that Clare had cooked with pears and celery in white wine and honey. 'Most unusual. Amazing combination of textures and flavours.'

Clare tried to play down the compliment—having been taught by the nuns at the convent that 'showing off' was not the 'done thing'—but she was delighted at his appreciation of all the time and effort she'd put into preparing the meal.

'Thanks, Fabian,' she said, going a little pinker than she was already, due in part to the heat of the oven and the two glasses of wine.

'That's a Frenchman for you,' said Jason, tucking in without commenting on the dish. 'It's like having the *Good Food Guide* man round, isn't it? ''An amazing combination of textures and flavours'',' he repeated, mimicking Fabian and adding a thick French accent.

Fabian stayed the night as Clare had suggested.

At two in the morning, Clare answered the call of

nature. 'Must be all that wine I drank last night,' she muttered to herself as she stumbled out of the bedroom and made her way to the bathroom. As she was returning she bumped into Fabian who had been awakened by the sound of Clare on the landing and had decided on a similar course of action.

Fabian, who normally slept in the buff, was wearing a specially bought pair of pyjamas. Clare, who had completely forgotten in the middle of the night that they had a house-guest, was wearing nothing.

'Oh!' she exclaimed in astonished embarrassment, making an unsuccessful but comical attempt to cover herself with her hands.

'It's all right, I'm a doctor,' joked Fabian, grinning amiably, before gallantly holding up his hands in front of his face.

'Not only a doctor, but a gentleman!' she said, appreciating the gesture, before scuttling back to her bedroom.

'Crikey!' she spluttered, trying to keep from laughing out loud.

Jason stirred sleepily. 'What's the matter?'

'Nothing you'd find funny,' she said, snuggling under the duvet.

The confrontation had given Fabian food for thought and when he returned to his bed he couldn't get to sleep for ages.

Images of the unclothed Clare kept disturbing his attempts at slumber. He'd taken it all in. Her beautiful breasts, her shapely buttocks and long legs, her flat stomach and the sexy triangle of golden-red hair. Clare in the nude would, he knew, be the subject of his fantasies for many restless nights to come.

He'd put up his hands to cover his eyes—and for that she'd called him a gentleman. But he'd kept his fingers open just enough to get a good eyeful of the delectable, naked Clare.

Not such a gentleman after all. Just a man.

CHAPTER TWO

FABIAN met Jason a few days later in the Quarry Bank Inn. It wasn't the pub they usually went to. In fact, Fabian had never been in it before.

The Quarry Bank was a deliberate choice by Jason.

'I don't want anyone we know seeing us talking,' he'd replied when Fabian had asked why they weren't meeting in the Builders' Arms as usual.

'This is all very clandestine,' he said to Jason, joining him at the bar of the Quarry Bank. 'And very mysterious. What's going on?'

'Let's get our drinks first and then we can take them to that table in the corner,' said Jason.

They did as Jason suggested and when they were seated, Fabian waited for his friend to speak first.

Jason looked cautiously around the room, checking once again that there was no one in the pub that he knew. 'Do you remember Carolyn Heston?' he asked.

Fabian was slightly taken aback. He'd been expecting this 'secret' conversation to be about Clare, particularly as Jason had hinted that they might be having fertility problems. That was the impression he'd gained on the night of the dinner.

'Carolyn Heston?' he repeated. The name had a very familiar ring to it. Within seconds a face to match the name came floating from his subconscious. A raven-haired beauty with a very independent mind…a girl who had been a medical student at the same time as Fabian and Jason.

A smile of recognition played on Fabian's lips.

'The girl who broke your heart,' he said, remembering the agonised talks he'd had with Jason on a regular basis as he'd poured out his distress to his friend. The misery, the anguish, the self-destroying torment that poor Jason had gone through as a result of falling for this girl had been heart-rending to witness. Fabian blamed Jason's exam failure and consequent loss of medical career on Carolyn.

'That's right,' said Jason, 'the girl who broke my heart. I met her last week.'

'You mean you bumped into her?' Fabian asked.

'No. She phoned me at work and we arranged to meet for lunch.' Jason stared guiltily into his beer. 'She's looking great.'

'What's she doing now?' asked Fabian. 'Is she still working in medicine?'

'Yes,' replied Jason. 'She's Dr Heston now.'

'Married?'

'No,' said Jason.

Fabian shifted in his chair and gazed around the room. The bar was beginning to get crowded with workers calling in for a quick drink on their way home—or with young people meeting before an evening out. He imagined that everyone in the bar knew why they were there. Everyone except him. He had no idea why Jason had arranged this covert meeting just to tell him he'd met up with a former girlfriend.

'Does Clare know that you've been seeing one of your exes?'

Jason stiffened. 'Hell, no! Why do you think I'm meeting you in here on the QT? Of course she doesn't know!'

Fabian was starting to become impatient with all this

cloak-and-dagger stuff. 'It's hardly a big deal, though, is it? Clare must know you had other girlfriends before you met her. I'm sure she doesn't think you came straight from a monastery. Tell her, for heaven's sake!'

'She's got a child,' said Jason.

'That's nice,' said Fabian.

'It's mine.'

Fabian stared at him, eyes wide in disbelief. 'Really?'

Jason nodded, a big grin spreading across his face. 'She's called Brook and she's seven years old.'

'Good grief! What a shock that must have been for you, to be told that.' Fabian paused. 'Of course, Carolyn may be lying and just hoping to get you lined up to pay child maintenance. Insist on a DNA test, whatever you do.'

'I'm sure she's mine,' said Jason, still grinning. 'Caro showed me a photograph. She looks just like me. And the dates fit. I worked it back from when Caro and I had that brief affair.'

Fabian remained silent, shaking his head slowly.

'You're wrong about her motives,' said Jason. 'She doesn't want child maintenance.'

'Then what does she want? You don't suddenly get in touch with the father of your child after seven years for no particular reason!'

'She says she wants to do the decent thing,' replied Jason. 'She felt guilty for not telling me about Brook because she thinks I have the right to know I'm a father. And Brook has the right to know who her father is. It's as simple as that.'

'It sounds anything but simple to me,' said Fabian. 'What, for instance, is Clare going to say about it?'

'I don't know,' confessed Jason. 'That's why I

wanted us to meet today. I need your advice and moral support. I just don't know what to do for the best. When I met Caro again it was as if we'd never been apart. All the same old feelings came flooding back. Here was I thinking I'd become cynical in my old age, the successful, quick-talking salesman—and yet with her I was tongue-tied.'

'So what happens next?' asked Fabian.

'I'm going over to her house soon to meet Brook. They live about forty miles away. Caro says she'll let me see Brook whenever I want.'

Fabian raised an eyebrow. 'Generous of her, after seven years.' He drained his glass. 'You asked my advice. My advice is that you tell Clare immediately. Tell her the whole story. There's nothing worse than deception in a relationship.'

Jason looked sheepish. 'I don't want to tell her. Not yet. I don't want to risk losing both of them. What if it doesn't work out with Caro?'

Fabian was dismayed. 'You're not seriously trying to get back with Carolyn Heston, are you?'

'Yes, if she'll have me,' said Jason. 'She's the only woman I've ever truly loved. I realise that now. She walked out once before because she didn't want me then—and there's no certainty that she'll want me now. But if there's the slightest chance for us to get back together I've got to go for it. If I tell Clare all this she'll, quite rightly, walk out on me. Then I could be left without either of them.'

'You know, Jason, you're acting like a complete louse.'

'That's what love does to you,' said Jason, giving Fabian a sly wink. 'Just wait till you fall heavily for someone. Then you'll know what I'm talking about.'

Jason downed the remains of his beer in one go. 'So,' he said, wiping his mouth with the back of his hand, 'can I count on you, old buddy?'

'To do what?'

'To back me up, give me a bit of support in the Clare direction until I know if there's a future for me with Caro?'

Fabian sighed. 'I suppose so. But I'm not going to be telling any lies for you, if that's what you think.'

Jason affected an innocent look. 'Would I do that?'

Clare was feeling thoroughly fed up. She'd had a bad day at The Hawthorns, her brother had phoned to say he'd lost his job, she'd forgotten to take anything out of the freezer that morning for their evening meal and would have to call at the supermarket on the way home, and, just as she was about to leave the surgery, the phone rang.

Before answering it, she poked her head round the door and said to the receptionist, 'I'm finishing now. Can you tell whoever it is to make an appointment for tomorrow? Or put the call through to one of the others. I think Dr Drumm's still here.'

The receptionist shrugged. 'She specifically asked for you, Dr Westwood. She's in a bit of a state. It's Gail Thewlis.'

Clare returned to her desk and picked up the phone.

'Dr Westwood,' she said.

'Oh, Doctor,' said a quavering voice. 'It's Gail Thewlis. I need help...'

'What's the matter, Gail? Are you feeling ill?' Clare felt her brain going into overdrive. The patient hadn't come in to see her as requested for the results of her blood test...and she and Fabian were still concerned

about the behaviour of Steve even though there was
nothing specific to report.

'It's not me, it's Steve. He's locked me in the house
and won't let me out.' She started to cry. 'He's locked
me in all week. To stop other men looking at me, he
says.'

'Have you called the police?' Clare asked. 'Dial 999,
for heaven's sake! Has he hit you or anything?'

'No, he hasn't hurt me,' she said between sobs. 'But
he says that if *he* can't have me, nobody can. I don't
know what to do.'

Clare heard a loud bang coming from the other end
of the phone. 'What was that?' she asked in alarm.

'He's come back!' Gail whispered, sounding terrified, and quickly replaced the receiver.

'Damn!' said Clare, fear creeping up her spine as
she envisaged the scene at the Thewlis's.

Without hesitating she dialled the police. Then she
ran into Fabian's room. He was working at his computer and looked up in surprise, smiling when he saw
who the intruder was. The smile froze on his lips when
she spoke.

'I think something awful is about to happen! We've
got to go over to Gail and Steve Thewlis's house. Now!
Let's go in your car because it's faster. I've just called
the police.'

Seeing the look on her face and her no-nonsense
attitude, he did as she asked. He closed down his computer and, picking up his medical bag, walked quickly
out of his room, following her to the car park.

As they were driving along, Fabian said, 'Tell me
what's happened. Has Steve gone berserk?'

'All I know is, Gail sounded terrified. She said that
Steve had locked her indoors all week and she was

phoning me for help. Then I heard this loud bang, like a door slamming. Gail said he'd come back and she put down the phone. Lord, I hope we're not too late.'

They turned into Unwin Avenue, the street where the Thewlises lived.

When they pulled up outside the house, they noticed something strange. The front door was wide open.

'Do you think the police did that?' Fabian asked. 'You know, kicked the door down?'

Clare stared at the open door, gripping and ungripping her hands nervously. 'I don't know. If the police are here, where's the police car?'

They walked towards the open door.

'I have a dreadful feeling in my bones that all is not well,' Clare said. As they reached the door they noticed that there were streaks of blood on the paintwork.

'Don't touch it,' Fabian said. 'Not even to see if it's wet.'

'Is anybody there?' he called out, putting a restraining hand on Clare. 'Don't go in,' he muttered. 'There might be someone with a weapon. Call the police on your mobile phone and find out where they are.'

As she was dialling, Fabian banged loudly on the front door, carefully avoiding the bloodstains. He called out Gail's and Steve's names, but there was no reply.

'The police are on their way,' said Clare. 'They said we shouldn't go in the building until they arrive.'

Fabian was sceptical. 'What if there's someone inside needing urgent medical attention?'

'Let's look through the downstairs windows,' suggested Clare.

They walked gingerly round the side of the house and peered in the windows. Everything seemed normal until they looked in the kitchen window. What they saw horrified them.

On the pine table in the centre of the room was a severed finger. Next to it was a meat cleaver. The table was covered in blood.

Clare gasped as her eyes lighted on the grisly spectacle. She turned to Fabian and buried her head in his chest. He held her tightly, feeling her whole body shaking uncontrollably. Adrenalin rushed to his aid enabling him to think quickly and clearly. Whoever that finger belonged to needed medical treatment as soon as possible.

'I'm going in,' he said to Clare. 'Gail may be lying unconscious somewhere in the house. There's not a moment to lose.'

'But what if *he's* in there? Shouldn't we wait for the police? I think I can hear the sirens.'

'In that case, you stand outside on the road and direct them to the house. I'm going to try and find Gail. Steve has probably run off—judging by the blood on the front door. He could be miles away by now.'

Clare, still stunned by their discovery, did as Fabian asked. When the police arrived she followed them into the house and called out anxiously to him, 'Fabian, where are you? Are you all right?'

A voice replied from upstairs. 'I'm fine,' he said. 'But I can't find any sign of either Gail or Steve. They've both vanished.'

The police, who'd arrived in three patrol cars, searched the house and garden. There was a trail of blood from the kitchen table, out through the front door and down the step. Then it stopped.

'She must have escaped,' said one of the officers. 'If

you've got a man with murderous intent chasing you, you can run like hell.'

'Oh, God,' said Clare, recalling the image of the severed finger.

'We must find her quickly,' Fabian told the officer.

'I've sent some of my men out searching for them,' he replied. 'They're checking first with the neighbours. If she's in the area we'll find her. Do you know if there was a motor vehicle on the property?' he asked.

'I've no idea,' said Clare. 'Do you know?' she asked Fabian.

He shook his head. 'It's not the kind of information we keep on a patient's medical records,' he replied dryly.

'The perpetrator might have been overcome with remorse and driven the victim to hospital,' suggested the police officer. A pretty unlikely scenario, he knew as well as anyone else—but, then, after fifteen years in the force, he'd learned to expect the unexpected.... Which was the next thing that happened.

'Sarg,' said a voice from the kitchen, 'you know this finger?'

'Put it in a specimen bag and label it,' he called back.

'That's not what I mean,' said the younger policeman. 'I don't think it's a woman's finger. It looks more like a man's. I'm almost certain it is, anyway.'

Clare and Fabian looked at each other in amazement.

'Does that mean Gail Thewlis chopped off her husband's finger?' whispered Clare in shocked amazement.

'We'd better pack it in ice,' Fabian said. 'There's an outside chance that if its owner is found in time it can be sewn on again.'

*   *   *

Clare and Fabian stayed at the house on Unwin Avenue for a further half-hour, but when they realised that there was nothing practical they could do, they decided to leave.

They were sitting in Fabian's car, putting on their seat belts, when a couple of policemen walked up the drive with Gail Thewlis between them.

Clare and Fabian returned to the house. They could hear the police sergeant cautioning Gail and telling her that she had the right to phone a solicitor if she wished to do so.

'Do you want to phone a solicitor?' he repeated.

'No, no!' she said, casting her eyes around the bloody scene. 'I haven't done anything. It was Steve. He came at me with a cleaver, saying he was going to chop me up! I ran out of the house and hid in a neighbour's garden until he drove away.'

'He drove away?' said the sergeant in disbelief. 'With his hand all chopped up?'

'What do you mean?' she asked.

The younger policeman held up the ice-packed specimen bag with its gruesome contents.

Gail blanched. 'What's that?'

'Somebody's finger, madam,' said the sergeant. 'Any idea whose?'

But no reply was forthcoming because Gail Thewlis had slumped senseless on the floor.

Steve was apprehended two miles away, collapsed over the steering-wheel of his car, clutching a teatowel to his bleeding hand. Clare and Fabian attended to his injuries, giving him emergency treatment before the ambulance arrived. They then went with him to St Margaret's Hospital, taking with them the severed finger packed in ice. Steve was rushed into surgery and underwent a three-hour operation to reattach it—it would be several days before the medics would know if the delicate microsurgery had been successful.

While he'd got his reluctant patient at the hospital, Fabian took the opportunity of speaking to a colleague in Neurology and mentioned his suspicions about Steve having a brain tumour. The neurologist said that when Steve was safely out of surgery he would arrange to give him a brain scan.

'His erratic behaviour and the headaches certainly ring alarm bells in that direction,' he told Fabian.

Gail was also admitted to St Margaret's Hospital—for observation. She didn't appear to have any physical injuries but she was in a very fragile state mentally.

Gail's version of events was that Steve had come home and found her on the telephone to Clare. He'd imagined she was phoning one of her 'lovers'. He'd threatened Gail that he'd cut off her fingers to stop her using the phone. She'd become very frightened and had believed he might carry out his threat when he'd gone to a drawer in the kitchen and pulled out the meat cleaver. She'd run out of the house and hidden behind a neighbour's garden wall. She'd heard him start up the car and drive away some minutes later but she had been too scared to return to the house in case he came back and locked her inside again. She'd decided to go to the next street and hide in a bus shelter for the time being. That's where she'd been when she'd been spotted by a policeman in a patrol car.

She'd had no idea that instead of cutting off her fingers Steve had chopped off one of his own.

*   *   *

'You were right,' said the neurologist a few days later. 'The scan showed a tumour in the right parietal lobe.'

'Is it operable?' Fabian asked.

'I think so. We won't know for sure until we do a craniotomy and take a biopsy sample, but it's much safer there than in the brain stem.'

'It's good news so far about his finger,' Fabian said.

'So I hear,' the neurologist said. 'Our Mr Thewlis is a lucky man…. Let's hope he's as lucky with his brain as he seems to be with his fingers.'

Gail Thewlis went home from her short stay in St Margaret's only to return there each day for the next three weeks visiting her husband. She'd noticed a remarkable change in him after the brain surgery.

'He seems to be his old self again—but a lot weaker of course,' she told Clare at the practice. 'And I was just so relieved that the tumour was benign. I can't wait to get him home and to start looking after him and helping to make him better. Those last months were so terrible—when I thought he'd gone funny in the head. It's a strange thing to say but I'm so glad it turned out to be a brain tumour—an operable one, of course—and not him going mental.'

Clare smiled reassuringly. 'It all worked out well in the end,' she said. 'But his finger could take months before he gets back any real feeling into it, if at all.'

'He knows that,' Gail said. 'He even managed a joke saying that it was a great pity because he'd always wanted to be a concert pianist.' She sighed. 'I'm glad he can laugh about it because I certainly can't. Not yet…maybe not ever. I'll always be haunted by the sight of that blood on the table and that finger in the bag.'

Clare handed Gail a prescription for some tranquillisers. 'Keep taking these for a little while longer,' she said. 'Soon you'll find you won't need them. Try to put that terrible image out of your mind and in time everything will get back to normal.'

On a Wednesday a few weeks later, Jason phoned Fabian before the start of morning surgery.

'Are you doing anything on Saturday?' he asked.

'As a matter of fact I'm going to Paris for the weekend to see my mother and sign a few papers,' replied Fabian.

At the other end of the phone he heard Jason utter a curse.

'Why do you ask?' Fabian enquired. 'Is there a problem? Clare hasn't mentioned anything about this Saturday.'

'She doesn't know, that's why!' Jason sounded agitated. 'I've arranged to go over to see Carolyn and Brook on Saturday. Clare was supposed to be staying the night with a relative but that's been cancelled because her aunt had to go into hospital. I thought you might have been able to help me out.'

'I don't see how I could have helped even if I was around,' said Fabian registering disapproval in his voice. He was most unhappy with the deceitful way his friend was behaving towards his medical colleague. In the short time he'd known Clare he'd become very fond of her and quickly realised that under her cheerful, forthright exterior, she was extremely sensitive and very vulnerable.

'What I'd done,' said Jason, 'was to tell Clare that I was going away on a business course. But I don't like leaving her alone at the weekend...'

'So you do have *some* honourable feelings left,' Fabian blurted out.

'Are you my friend or not?' Jason asked.

'I'm not sure at this particular moment,' replied Fabian frostily.

'Look, this thing with Caro, it will be settled one way or another in the very near future. Possibly this weekend. If she kicks me out then I'll put it all behind me, I promise. I'll be all lovey-dovey with Clare again and she needn't get hurt unnecessarily. You don't want her to be hurt, do you?'

'Of course not!' Fabian was so irritated that he wanted to slam the phone down. But he knew that wouldn't help the situation. Instead he said, 'What is it you want me to do?'

'I just thought it would be great if you could go to Paris another time and instead ask Clare out for a meal on Saturday. It would take her mind off me not being there, for a start. As you probably guess, I'm feeling more than a little guilty about all this. So, it will be my treat...the best food, the best wine,' he said, 'and I'll pay for everything.'

'What with?' said Fabian. 'Thirty pieces of silver?'

Fabian had decided he was having nothing to do with Jason's duplicity. But by lunchtime he'd changed his mind.

He was at the Builders' Arms with Clare and Sam. It was obvious to Fabian that Clare hadn't the slightest notion that her boyfriend was deceiving her. It was also obvious that if he didn't step in with some arrangement along the lines that Jason had suggested, Clare might become suspicious and discover the truth.

'He said he'd only signed up for this business course

because I was going to be away this weekend,' said Clare crossly. 'You'd think he'd cancel it, wouldn't you, now that I'm going to be at home?'

'You should fix up something else,' suggested Sam. 'You can come round to my place on Saturday if you're stuck for something to do. My flat could do with a good spring-clean.'

'Thanks for nothing!' said Clare, chortling into her lemonade. 'I've an aversion to bachelor flats. They're normally disgusting places with grease two inches thick on all the cooking surfaces.'

'Mine's not like that!' protested Fabian.

Clare leaned conspiratorially in his direction. 'In that case, I'll come round to your place.'

Fabian scraped his throat. 'I'm going to Paris to see my mother this weekend.'

'That sounds an even better offer,' said Sam, grinning broadly.

They both looked at Fabian expectantly.

'You're very welcome to come along,' he said. 'There's a small amount of business I have to see to but, apart from that, my time—and Paris—will be at your disposal.'

Clare clapped her hands delightedly like a small child. 'Great! But are you sure, Fabian? I'd be thrilled to come. I've never been to Paris and I'm always going on at Jason to take me.' She paused for a second. 'But what about your mother? Won't she be disappointed not to have you to herself?'

Fabian shrugged. 'She's seen plenty of me over the years. It was just the two of us for a long time. I'm sure a weekend of sharing me with someone else won't bother her. And she loves cooking, so it will give her an added incentive to show off her cordon bleu.'

'You'd better warn her that I'm just a work colleague,' said Clare, 'or she might be hearing wedding
bells inside her head. I know what mothers of sons are
like. The moment my mother sees my brother with a
new girlfriend, she's out round the shops choosing a
wedding outfit.'

'I think she knows me better than that,' replied
Fabian. 'Matrimony is something neither of us are too
keen on after the experience she had with my father.
That episode was enough to put anyone off marriage
for life.'

Nevertheless, Fabian did take the precaution of phoning his mother and explaining that he'd be bringing a
female colleague with him, and that he and the female
colleague would be sleeping in separate bedrooms and
that they were not romantically linked.

As he spoke the words, he felt a tinge of regret. If
he was going to be romantically linked with someone,
he couldn't think of anyone he'd rather it would be
than Clare.

He was very ambivalent. On the one hand he hoped
that Carolyn *was* going to reject Jason and that he'd
return to Clare—a scenario that would be in Clare's
best interests. On the other hand, a little bit of Fabian
hoped that Jason and Carolyn hit it off, leaving Clare
available for him.

On the flight to Paris, he couldn't resist trying to
find out more about Clare's feelings for Jason and how
serious about him she was.

'Do you think you'll marry Jason?' he asked.

Clare pondered for a moment. 'Probably,' she said.
'He reminds me so much of my brother—feckless, ca-
sual, unreliable but a real charmer. It wouldn't surprise

me to learn that he's planning some outlandish scheme
before he proposes. Choosing some fantastically romantic location. There'll be none of the dropping-
down-on-one-knee stuff for Jason. He'll do it differently, I can assure you.'

She paused, narrowing her eyes as if deep in thought.
'You're not in on this, are you?'

'What are you talking about?'

'This weekend. It isn't all an elaborate scheme to get
me over to Paris and up the Eiffel Tower, so that Jason
can appear from behind a pillar and pop the question?
I wouldn't put it past him to concoct a plan like that!'
She looked coyly under her eyelashes at Fabian.

He couldn't bear to see the innocent, trusting gleam
in her eyes, knowing what he knew. Knowing that, far
from planning a romantic proposal in Paris, Jason was
otherwise occupied with another woman.

'No,' said Fabian, curtly. 'I can almost guarantee
that isn't going to happen.'

'Ah,' said Clare, settling down in her airline seat,
'you don't know Jason!'

Oh, but I do, said Fabian to himself.

CHAPTER THREE

AS THE taxi dropped them outside a house in one of the most attractive areas of Paris, Clare gasped in admiration.

'Your mother must be loaded!' she said. Tact had never been her strong point.

Fabian laughed at her outspoken remark. He found the way she spoke her thoughts out loud very endearing and not at all offensive or rude.

'Lack of money was never a problem in my parents' marriage,' he said as they approached the steps up to the nineteenth-century townhouse. 'The problem was lack of love. I would much rather have grown up poor, but loved. Loved by both parents, that is.'

He rang the doorbell and then, without waiting for his ring to be answered, used his own set of keys to open the front door. He led the way into a cool, uncluttered hall with black-and-white tiles, which gave it the appearance of a Dutch painting.

'Mama, we're here!' he called out.

Clare heard a woman's voice murmur something from behind a closed door at the end of the hallway. The door opened and Mrs Drumm appeared.

She was slim and petite and wore an elegant, dark-blue, pencil-thin skirt and a toning twin-set in fine cotton. Her mid-brown hair was beautifully styled. Clare thought she was the embodiment of the word 'chic'.

Fabian's mother held out her arms to greet them, first

reaching up on tiptoe to kiss her son and then enclosing Clare's hands in her own.

'You must be Dr Westwood,' she said in greeting. 'Welcome to Paris. My son tells me it is your first visit.'

She smiled warmly and Clare thought how lovely she was. With her exquisite bone structure and beautiful skin she looked like a woman who in her younger days could have been a fashion model. Her eyes were like her son's, deep brown with long, black lashes. But that was where the resemblance ended. Seeing them together, Clare would never have picked them out as being mother and son. Fabian must take after his father for his looks, mused Clare. The father he hates.

'Please call me Clare, Mrs Drumm.'

'And you must call me Marie-Paul,' said Fabian's mother. 'My son will show you to your room and then come down to the sitting room where I shall have tea waiting for you. I know how you British like your cup of tea.'

'I'd love a cup of tea, Mrs Drumm,' said Clare, adding hastily, 'I mean, Marie-Paul.'

Fabian took Clare's bag and made his way up the stairs. She followed closely behind. The room he took her to was fresh and dainty, with choice antiques all around. The walls were painted in the palest blue wash, and the duvet cover and curtains were in white embroidered cotton edged with antique lace.

She walked over to the tall casement window. The view over Paris was breathtaking. She gasped in delight and, stepping back a pace, bumped up against Fabian who was now standing behind her. He put his arms around her waist to steady her.

'Sorry!' she said. 'Did I step on your foot?'

'No,' he replied, his hands still on her waist, her back resting against his chest.

'It's a fabulous view,' said Clare huskily.

It must be the Parisian atmosphere getting to her, she thought, as a warm languor took possession of her. She could feel the heat radiating through his clothes and the imprint of his body of hers. She remembered being this close to him not all that long ago, on the day she'd recoiled in shock on seeing Steve Thewlis's severed finger. Fabian had held her close to him, comforting her, and she recalled the masculine scent of him, raw and sensual.

'Yes, it is,' he replied, his voice equally husky, 'a fabulous view.'

She became aware of the gentle pressure of his hands becoming firmer, harder. She didn't move away as she knew she should have done. She was playing with fire. It must be Paris that's making me act like this, she told herself as she turned slowly towards him and lifted her face to his.

He reacted without hesitation, grasping her head in both hands and bringing his mouth down on hers. He kissed her passionately, tilting her head over his arm.

Her body trembled as she responded willingly. They kissed, and went on kissing. He held her tighter to keep her trembling in check, as if to absorb it and make it his own. Then, as if scalded, he let go, shocked at his own impetuous behaviour.

He opened his mouth to speak but she put a finger to his lips.

'Don't say it,' she said. 'Don't say you're sorry and all that stuff.'

He ran a hand through his hair in a nervous gesture. 'All right, I won't.'

'Blame it on Paris,' she said. 'City of romance and all that kind of thing. It had me under its spell for a few minutes there.' She laughed brightly. 'Better not tell Jason about it, though, when he pops out from behind that pillar on the Eiffel Tower!'

Her humour had defused the tension of the situation and Fabian was able to relax. 'No, we'd better not tell him,' he agreed and, smiling at her, walked out leaving her alone in the bedroom. Leaving her alone to relive the delicious sensation of his kiss.

Her emotions were a tortured mixture of guilt and pleasure. She knew she shouldn't have done it, but she was glad she had. His mouth had felt unashamedly delicious, his kiss one of the best she'd ever had. And yet, wasn't that often the way with a first kiss? She tried to think back to the first time she'd kissed Jason. Had she experienced this same heady, body-tingling sensation? Probably, she admitted. The first time was always special. That first passionate touch, that first taste of someone new.

She ran some cold water into the washbasin in the *en suite* bathroom and splashed it onto her face. It wouldn't happen again, she was pretty sure of it. Their impulsive, spur-of-the-moment embrace had taken them both by surprise and, judging by the embarrassed look on Fabian's face, she could almost guarantee that her medical colleague would be going out of his way to ensure it didn't happen again. Fabian was a loyal friend to Jason, she knew that. And *she* was a loyal girlfriend. What had happened was out of character for both of them.

She dried her face, brushed her hair and put on a flick of lipstick.

'Time for that cup of tea, you hussy,' she told her mirror image.

Tea in a silver pot, and china cups and saucers, were set out on a low table in the sunny sitting room. There was also a mouthwatering chocolate cake. Fabian's mother poured the tea after enquiring about Clare's preference.

'No milk, thanks,' she replied. 'That cake looks delicious. Fabian tells me you're a very good cook.'

'I do love cooking,' she admitted. 'It's what I used to do before I got married. I was a caterer and ran my own business.' She turned to face her son. 'Fabian, would you cut Clare a slice of gateau?'

Fabian did as his mother asked and handed her a slice of cake on a dainty china plate. As Clare took the plate from him their eyes met. She was amused that he didn't hold her gaze for long, quickly dropping his eyes to her lips and then, as if embarrassed to be seen looking at the mouth he'd so recently covered with his own, to the slice of chocolate cake.

'Tell me more about your catering business, Marie-Paul,' said Clare in an attempt to cover for Fabian who seemed to have lost the power of speech.

'I used to employ three others and we specialised in business lunches and presentations and that kind of thing. That's how I met my husband. We had a contract with his company and we used to do very posh lunches in the boardroom for their monthly meetings.'

At the mention of his father, Fabian looked uncomfortable. But his mother continued as if she hadn't noticed.

'I suppose you might say he married me for my cooking. Although I wasn't bad-looking, so it might have been a combination of looks and food.'

Clare cast around the room to see if there were any photographs of Fabian's father. She imagined he must have similar looks to his son because Fabian certainly hadn't taken after his mother. But there were no photographs of any description. Quite unlike the living room of her family home where every available surface was covered with pictures of the entire family in various stages from babyhood onwards.

'Is your husband still alive?' she asked. She sensed Fabian stiffening but she held her course and looked directly at Mrs Drumm.

'Yes, he is,' she replied. 'But, as I'm sure Fabian will have told you, we were divorced many years ago. He lives in London with his second wife.'

'What a shame,' said Clare. 'Not about him marrying again... I mean what a shame your marriage didn't work out.'

'Yes,' she said quietly. 'A great shame.'

Without meaning to, Clare had caused an awkward silence to fall around them. The sound of clinking china cups was all that could be heard for a few, very long moments...moments that seemed like hours.

'So, you're going to be showing Clare some of the sights of Paris, Fabian?' said his mother, to break the silence. 'Where will you take her this afternoon? La Tour Eiffel?'

A quirky smile crossed his lips. 'I suppose we'd better get that out of the way. Then Clare can relax once she knows that no one's going to appear from behind a pillar and propose marriage to her.'

'*Pardon?*' said his mother, creasing her brow. 'Someone is going to propose marriage to Clare? Is it you, Fabian?'

Clare burst out laughing. 'He's teasing me, Marie-Paul. Fabian is certainly not planning on proposing to me!'

Mrs Drumm ran her eyes appraisingly over Clare for a second or two, alighting on her tumbling red tresses and her large blue eyes.

'That's a pity,' she said.

Fabian and Clare spent the afternoon doing the kind of touristy things that he would normally have avoided like the plague... A trip down the Seine in a *bateau mouche*, mingling with the crowds on the riverside *quais*, having a (very expensive) drink in one of the pavement cafés on the Champs Elysée...and, of course, going up the Eiffel Tower.

'Tomorrow I'll take you to Montmartre,' said Fabian as they surveyed the whole of Paris from the top of the tower.

'This is wonderful,' she said, gazing at the city spread out beneath them. 'I know it's corny and clichéd and all that kind of thing, but you must admit that this is an experience which takes some beating!'

Fabian found her childlike enthusiasm captivating. In a world so full of cynics and scoffers, Clare's genuine joy was infectious. He stood next to her at the railing and began to look at the city he knew so well with fresh eyes. He slipped an arm around her waist.

'Not disappointed, then?' he asked.

'Goodness me, no,' she replied breathlessly.

'I mean about the proposal.'

Clare looked behind her suspiciously. Fabian could have kicked himself. Without meaning to, he had raised her hopes that this was, in fact, a prearranged ploy by Jason to get her up the tower.

'You're kidding me, aren't you?' She looked into his eyes, searching for the truth.

He dropped his arm from her waist. 'I promise you, Jason isn't in Paris. So you can relax.'

'Oh,' she said, slightly crestfallen. 'I'm just too romantic for my own good, that's my problem. It's just a bit of a dream I had, that's all.' She stared out over the city and its spiralling *arrondissements*.

Fabian felt an inexplicable urge to make her dreams come true. He gripped the handrail and willed himself to think of something else—realising that if he wasn't careful he'd end up proposing to her himself!

'I suggest we return to the house now,' he said. 'We can have a shower and change and then I'll take you out somewhere special for dinner.'

'Will your mother come along as well?' Clare asked. 'I think she's lovely and it would be great to have a nice long chat with her.'

'I'll ask her but I've a feeling she'll decline. She's not a great one for restaurants. She'd rather cook something herself at home.'

'But won't she mind us going out and leaving her? I feel it's a bit rude of us. And surely she'll want to have a nice long chat with you—even if she doesn't want one with me?' Clare was conscious of the fact that she'd invited herself along on Fabian's home visit.

'She won't mind at all. I often go out with Parisian friends when I'm over…and I'll make sure I get to have some private time with her. There are some papers she needs me to look at and some documents to sign. But that shouldn't take too long.'

Back at the house, Clare showered and changed into fresh clothes for the evening—black trousers and an

emerald green top. She'd also brought a white cash-
mere cardigan which she slung over her shoulders as a
protection against the cooler night air.

Marie-Paul waved them off, instructing them both to
have a lovely time.

They strolled along the wide boulevard lined with
plane trees towards Fabian's favourite brasserie—one
that he assured her was 'not full of tourists'.

She linked her arm in his and gave it a squeeze.
'What an old snob you are, Monsieur le Docteur.'

They turned off the main boulevard and dived into
a maze of small side streets. Piano music spilled out
of one of the bistros as they walked past.

'Not far to go now,' said Fabian when Clare told
him she felt totally and completely lost.

The restaurant he guided her to was quite unprepos-
sessing on the outside and not much more impressive-
looking on the inside. But it had an indefinable ambience and Fabian assured her it served 'the best food
and wine in town'. It appeared on first sight to be full
but the waiter, recognising Fabian, directed them to a
place in the corner.

'Just as well you booked,' said Clare, as the waiter
removed the réservé sign from their table.

As they tucked into delicious entrecôte steaks accompanied by salad and a red wine of perfect temperature and taste, Clare complimented him on his choice
of restaurant. 'That's the marvellous thing about coming to Paris with a genuine Parisian,' she said. 'You
know all the special places—and it's great being with
someone who speaks the lingo like a native.'

He looked at her across the candle flame and realised
that to onlookers they must seem like lovers. He was
enjoying her company enormously… If he had a

'dream girl', which of course he hadn't, Clare would come very close. And, feeling the way he did, he had a heavy heart weighed down by guilt. Guilt because he knew something that she didn't and which, through loyalty to his friend, he couldn't tell her. But didn't he also owe loyalty to Clare as a friend and colleague?

'You're very quiet,' she said, pouring herself a second glass of Chambertin.

'I was thinking about Jason,' admitted Fabian. 'I know him a lot better than you do, I would imagine.'

'Oh, I know him pretty well,' replied Clare.

Fabian trod carefully. 'What would you do if you discovered he was, say, having an affair?'

Clare laughed. 'Jason? Who'd have him? That's what he always says to me!'

'So you have talked about…that kind of thing?'

'I certainly have,' replied Clare, unfazed. 'And he knows that if there's any monkey business he's out! That flat belongs to me and he knows full well that he'd be kicked out of the door, quickly followed by his suitcase and medical samples.' She laughed at the image she'd created, an image she felt certain would never become reality.

'You're very trusting,' said Fabian quietly.

'And you're very cynical,' she replied. 'Just because you had a bad experience with your parents' marriage doesn't mean that all loving relationships are doomed.' She picked up the menu. 'Now, which of these desserts do you recommend? It's all French to me.'

Later that night, when Clare had undressed, washed and settled down under the duvet, she heard noises downstairs. She sat up in bed and realised it was the sound of raised voices.

She put on her lacy cotton dressing-gown and opened her bedroom door a crack. There was definitely some fierce arguing going on downstairs in the living room or kitchen. She didn't recognise a word of it as it was in French and spoken very quickly, but she recognised the voices. It was Fabian and Marie-Paul shouting and screaming at each other. Every now and then she heard banging, like the sound of a fist being thumped on a table. Suddenly a door downstairs opened and slammed shut. Then she heard footsteps racing up the stairs.

She quickly closed her door and retreated back to bed. She didn't want Fabian to know that she'd been eavesdropping on something that was obviously very private.

The next morning at breakfast, Marie-Paul was nowhere to be seen. Fabian was in the kitchen-cum-breakfast room on his own.

'Freshly squeezed orange juice, croissants and coffee?' he asked.

'Yes, please,' she replied. There wasn't anything about Fabian's demeanour to give any clue about the noisy quarrel she had overheard the previous night. 'Is your mother joining us for *petit déjeuner*?' asked Clare, throwing in the only French words she could remember off-hand.

'No,' said Fabian. 'She has a migraine and sends her apologies.'

After breakfast Fabian took Clare, as promised, to Montmartre. They rode the underground to the Métro Abbesses station and set off through narrow streets towards the Sacré Coeur, the familiar Byzantine basilica resembling a sumptuously-iced wedding cake. On the way they mingled with the hordes of tourists, most of whom appeared to be heading, along with Clare and Fabian, in the direction of the old village square.

Accordion music was in the air, coming from no discernible location but adding an authentic bohemian touch to the occasion. In the little square, west of the Sacré Coeur, Clare spied a forest of wooden easels amid the hectic bustle of street artists and a clutch of trendy little restaurants, all competing for the visitors' money.

They approached the basilica and joined the dozens of others who were walking up the long flights of steps to the dome.

'I'd forgotten what a superb view this is,' said Fabian in grudging admiration.

Clare agreed it was a great view. 'Better than the Eiffel Tower, I think,' she said. 'But don't quote me on that.'

Back in the square they sat outside one of the pavement cafés and ordered coffee. Fabian hadn't been very conversational all morning and Clare, realising it might have something to do with last night's shouting match, decided to keep her conversation and observations to a minimum.

They sat in companionable silence and watched people having their portraits sketched. Each subject was surrounded by small, nosy groups. Dozens of pairs of eyes swivelled from the faces of the sitters to the portraits and back. Many of the onlookers were giving a running commentary on the work in progress. The artists were swift and professional, unrolling the paper, capturing the main features and then covering the finished portrait with plastic and rolling it up with a flourish.

All this activity kept Fabian and Clare amused and occupied—and it also meant that they didn't need to speak on a personal level. But eventually Clare felt the urge to say something about the scene she'd witnessed the previous night and so, when she'd finished her coffee, she said, 'Is everything OK with you, Fabian? I heard a lot of shouting last night. I became worried. And you seem a little preoccupied today.'

He remained silent for ages, almost as if he hadn't heard what she'd said.

'Fabian?' she repeated.

'I wondered if you'd heard us last night,' he said. 'I wasn't going to say anything but now I suppose I have to offer an explanation.'

Clare smiled brightly. 'No you don't,' she said. 'If you want to keep it to yourself that's your privilege.'

He said nothing but just looked around the square as if he *were* going to keep it to himself. When he turned to face her, she saw a look of thunder.

'I'll tell you,' he said. 'I need to tell someone.' His voice was low and tremulous.

'Good grief, Fabian, whatever's the matter? Have you had some bad news?'

'In a way,' he replied. 'To start with, I've just discovered I've been left half a million pounds.'

'Wow!' said Clare. 'That's the kind of bad news I like!'

'There's more to it,' he replied solemnly. 'Much more. My mother gave me the news about the legacy last night. It was from a man, an American, who was a friend of the family, she said. I'd never heard of this man, George Merrick, until my mother told me last night that he's left me all this money. He's also left her a considerable sum.'

'That's very odd,' said Clare. 'You'd think at least you'd have heard his name mentioned before, wouldn't you?'

'Precisely. I asked her who the hell he was. At first she was coy about it, saying he was someone she'd known through her catering business. Someone who'd been based in Paris and also in the construction industry like my father.'

He paused and gave a hollow laugh. 'Or should I say the man I'd always believed was my father!'

'Oh,' said Clare quietly.

'I finally got the truth from her. She had a brief affair with this George Merrick and became pregnant. My father—or should I say my mother's husband—said he would forgive the infidelity if she would have the baby adopted at birth. At first my mother agreed to this. But when I was born she couldn't give me up.'

'I wonder why she didn't just pretend that you were his child? Would he ever have known that you weren't his baby? They didn't have DNA tests in those days, just a blood test —and that was never one hundred per cent reliable. There might have been a small chance that you could have been his child if she was still sleeping with him. It would have saved a lot of heartache for all concerned, that's for sure.'

Fabian stared blankly ahead of him. 'He was sterile, my mother said…as a result of radium treatment as a young man. When they married they both knew the marriage would be childless—and my mother had told him that she wasn't concerned about it. She had her catering business and their lives were fulfilled without a family. It was only after she gave birth that she experienced overwhelming maternal feelings and knew she could never give up her baby.'

Clare looked at Fabian. 'And she told you all this last night?'

'Yes. So now can you understand why I lost my temper and started shouting at her? I'm thirty-two years old and have only just discovered who my real father is! How could she have kept the truth from me for so long? I was blazing mad.' He paused for a brief moment. 'She said that she would have told me eventually. But I just don't believe her.'

'That's a bit harsh,' said Clare, feeling some sympathy for Marie-Paul. 'It must be very difficult choosing the right time to tell someone that kind of news.'

'She said she nearly told me at the time of their divorce. But she didn't. I really don't think she would ever have told me. It was only the fact that I'd been left this enormous legacy by this man George Merrick which made it inevitable that the truth would have to come out. I can't tell you how angry all this has made me.'

Clare reached out and put a comforting hand on his shoulder. His muscles were clenched in a tight knot. 'I think I *do* know how angry it made you. I heard you thumping the table pretty forcefully last night.'

Fabian shuddered at the memory. 'That was after she told me that she'd written me a letter and placed it with her will. I would have found out all about it after she had died. She seemed to think that this made the whole deception acceptable! Can you imagine me reading the letter and coping with that kind of news at a time of mourning her loss? That's why I thumped the table!'

He put a hand to his shoulder and covered hers. They sat in silence holding hands and staring into space. After a short while she gave his hand a squeeze.

'At least you know why your father—I mean your

mother's husband—always treated you so coldly. In a strange way don't you find that helpful? And he did behave in a decent way standing by your mother and supporting her financially if not emotionally.'

Fabian sighed. 'Maybe.'

'I wonder why she didn't get a divorce earlier and marry George Merrick?'

'He was already married, she told me. But he always kept in touch with her and took an interest in what I was doing over the years. She'd been secretly sending him photographs and letters. You think you at least know your own flesh and blood—and then something like this happens and you discover that your own mother has deceived you all your life. She'd have made a brilliant wartime spy!'

'Perhaps as a little girl she was in the Resistance?' suggested Clare, giving his hand another squeeze. 'The deception becomes kind of romantic if you think of it like that.' She raised her eyebrows at him.

'I'll try and think of it in that light,' he said, a smile on his lips for the first time in ages.

'And once you're over your righteous anger you've got a cool half-million to help take away the pain of deception.'

'I suppose so.'

'What'll you spend it on? A new sports car? An upgraded apartment...a holiday in Las Vegas? Perhaps all three?'

'Perhaps all three,' agreed Fabian. He put money on the table for the coffees and then they rose to leave. They walked, still hand in hand, across the busy square.

'Thanks for listening,' he said.

'That's what friends are for,' she said. 'Let's be the

kind of friends who never have any secrets from each other. Agreed?'

'Agreed,' said Fabian, before realising that he was already keeping a secret from her. The secret of Jason and Carolyn.

CHAPTER FOUR

Two days later it was Clare who was thumping on Fabian's desk in furious anger.

'You knew, didn't you? You bloody well knew!' she stormed at him.

Fabian took a deep breath. 'What's happened?' he asked calmly.

'Jason is leaving me and setting up home with some woman who has his child! He fixed it all up at the weekend. The weekend *we* were in Paris. And, what's more, he tells me that *you* knew all about it!' Her eyes were blazing and her skin had taken on a colour to rival her red hair. But underneath the bravado he could sense the hurt and pain she was undoubtedly feeling.

He lowered his eyes in shame. He *had* known all about it and she was right to feel betrayed by him— just as she felt betrayed by Jason. But what could he have done? Should he have spoken out?

'I'm sorry' was all he could bring himself to say to her.

'Sorry!' she shouted at him.

She noticed how, when she raised her voice, his eyes darted towards the door.

'Don't worry, Dr Drumm, I've closed the door so that the rest of the medical centre won't hear what a fraud you are! Pretending to be my friend and confidant while all along you knew what was going on behind my back.'

Fabian opened his hands palms upwards in a gesture

of futility. 'You're right, I did know. But Jason is also my friend and I was sworn to secrecy—for the immediate future. I made him promise that he'd tell you after this weekend when he'd made up his mind about Carolyn. If it's any comfort to you, I told him I thought he was behaving like a complete louse.'

'I bet that really upset him, you saying that! I bet it made him quake in his boots being called a nasty name by his loyal friend. It seems that I'm the only one who *hasn't* got a loyal friend!'

Clare put her hands up to her face and sat down heavily in a chair next to Fabian's desk.

Her anger seemed to have disappeared as quickly as it had arisen, to be replaced by an overwhelming desire to weep.

He jumped up and went to her, putting his arms around her and raising her to her feet. Then he held her close to him and let her cry on his shoulder.

'We've both been deceived,' he said softly, 'and by people we thought we could trust. Me by my mother, you by Jason. We're the wronged ones, we're the victims—so let's not fight with each other about it.'

He placed his hand around her head and stroked her silky hair, slowly and soothingly. They stood like that for several minutes. As they pulled away slightly they looked into each other's eyes.

And then she knew. She knew that ever since she'd met Fabian her relationship with Jason had become meaningless. The man she dreamed about, fantasised about and yearned to touch her, was not Jason. It was Fabian. And although she loved the idea of being proposed to by Jason on top of the Eiffel Tower, even she had to admit that the engagement would probably have been broken before a wedding date was fixed. Ever since she'd met Fabian she'd realised, deep down in her soul, that she would never have married Jason.

What had so upset her was the shock of Jason's news and the depth of his deception.

She took a deep breath and let it out slowly. Her anger had evaporated and in its place was another emotion. She reached out and lightly touched his lips with her fingers.

'What are you thinking about?' he asked huskily, aroused by her mood change.

'I was remembering Paris and how nice it was,' she said, staring at his mouth and recalling the delicious sensation of his kiss.

His lips grazed the side of her cheek. 'Any particular moment in mind?'

'Yes.' She turned her head slightly so that her lips met his. His kiss was just as sensational as when he'd kissed her the first time. So much for that theory, she thought as she experienced the same rush of excitement surge through her body as it had in Paris. This time, however, she was able to enjoy the pleasurable sensation without the added guilt. Now she was a free agent and not somebody else's girlfriend.

They were interrupted by the intercom.

'Are you ready for your first patient, Dr Drumm?' enquired the receptionist's disembodied voice.

They untangled themselves from their clinch and grinned sheepishly at each other. Clare resisted the urge to giggle, knowing that the sound would carry back to the reception desk.

Fabian cleared his throat before saying, 'Yes, I'm ready now.'

'I'll be getting back to my room,' said Clare in a whisper, creeping quietly to the door. She didn't know why she was acting in this clandestine way after they'd been interrupted in mid-embrace. She felt like a naughty schoolgirl and wanted to burst into peals of laughter.

Fabian found himself grinning inanely as he straightened his tie and smoothed his ruffled hair. It was like a scene from a French farce, he mused. As Clare let herself out of his room she blew him a kiss. It made him feel good. In fact the whole encounter had cheered him up no end. It had taken his mind off his own betrayal—and it held out the prospect of a closer relationship with Clare, a woman he found extremely desirable.

By the time his first patient walked into his room, Fabian Drumm was one happy and contented man.

Fabian and Clare started dating. They decided it would be sensible not to rush headlong into a sexual relationship. 'I don't want you to think I'm falling for you on the rebound,' said Clare when they were discussing the issue.

'Indeed, no,' agreed Fabian who was certainly not a man who rushed headlong into anything. On the other hand, he wasn't quite sure how long he could stand to wait until the relationship became more physically intense. He was desperate to sleep with her…but he made a supreme effort to put those thoughts to the back of his mind.

Clare had awakened in him feelings he hadn't known existed. He was now, for the first time in his life, considering what it would be like to be married. For him it was probably a combination of meeting Clare and, at the same time, learning about his own parentage. She'd been right when she'd pointed out that he now knew that his father was not the man who'd brought him up and because of this, he might find it helpful in understanding why he'd been treated so coldly by the man he'd called 'Daddy'.

He was slowly beginning to accept that none of it was his fault and that the suffering he'd experienced as a rejected child was, although not forgivable, at least understandable. And slowly he was losing his jaundiced attitude towards marriage and all that it entailed. There were some people, he realised, who could commit themselves to each other on a long-term basis and who could bring children into the world who were wanted and loved by both parents...people who stayed together because they loved each other and not because they felt obliged to stick it out until the children had grown up and then get the divorce they probably should have got years before.

After they'd been going out together for a few weeks, he was round at Clare's flat one evening and sensed that tonight was probably going to be the night they would make love for the first time. She had cooked him a special meal, served by candlelight, accompanied by a very expensive bottle of wine.

Fabian admired her choice.

She was secretly delighted that he'd appreciated the huge chunk of salary she'd spent on it. 'I couldn't give any old plonk to a man who's half-French, could I?'

The expensive wine would have been totally wasted on Jason, who always said he preferred wine bottles with screw-tops because they were easier to open.

Fabian held up the bottle and looked at the wine that was remaining. He estimated there were still a couple of glasses left. 'Seems a shame to leave it,' he said, regretfully, 'but I don't want to get breathalized on the

way home.' He hadn't said it with any ulterior motive
in mind. Or perhaps he had. He couldn't quite decide…

But he was very happy when she said, 'You could
stay the night and then we could finish the bottle.' She
smiled at him across the empty plates and the flickering
candle flame. 'I've got a spare toothbrush.'

He entwined his fingers with hers. For what seemed
an eternity they looked at each other. She couldn't take
her eyes off him and neither could he take his off her.
In the subdued lighting she could hear his breathing,
shallow and uneven.

'Is that a yes, then?' she said, almost in a whisper.

'It's a yes please,' he said, equally softly. He rose
from the table, lifting her to her feet at the same time.
He pulled her to him and kissed her roughly and with
all the pent-up passion in him.

'Let's go to bed now,' he said. 'Forget about the
wine.'

They were kissing each other hungrily and at the
same time moving towards the bedroom when the
doorbell rang. A harsh, insistent ring.

'Shall we ignore it?' said Clare, her desire for Fabian
clouding everything else.

'It's your doorbell, your decision,' said Fabian between kisses. He hoped she would ignore it, his need
for her was so great.

The doorbell rang again.

'It's probably a drunk pressing the wrong button,'
she said, pulling him towards the bed.

It rang again. Whoever was doing the pressing was
now leaning on the button full time. The noise went
on and on. It was impossible to ignore.

'Damn it,' she snarled. 'I'll have to go and see
what's going on.'

She pressed the intercom linking her second-floor flat with the main front door. 'Yes,' she said, crossly, 'who is it?'

'It's me,' replied a groggy voice, 'Simon.'

Clare put a hand over the intercom microphone. 'It's my brother,' she hissed. 'He *never* comes round. It must be something urgent—I wonder what's happened?''

'You'll only find out by asking him,' said Fabian, stating the obvious.

'What is it, Simon?' she asked.

'Let me in and then I'll tell you,' he replied in a slurred voice.

Clare had gone chalk-white. She pressed the door release. 'I wonder what's the matter?' she said, a stricken look crossing her face. 'I wonder if it's my parents?'

'He sounded drunk to me,' said Fabian.

'Yes,' she said. 'Perhaps he's just drunk. Let's hope so anyway.'

They stepped outside her flat and stood in the passageway waiting for Simon to arrive. The lift doors opened and a bedraggled young man covered in blood virtually fell out of it.

'What the hell's happened to you?' said Clare, rushing over to him. 'Have you been in a road accident?'

'Yeah, that's right,' said Simon, 'a road accident.'

They took him inside and sat him down on a kitchen chair. Clare and Fabian both examined him. His injuries seemed to be mainly to his head and face.

'When was your last tetanus injection?' Fabian asked him.

'Couple of years ago,' replied Simon slowly.

Clare confirmed her brother's reply. 'I gave it to him myself.'

Fabian shone a penlight into Simon's eyes, checking them for signs of progressive brain damage. 'Pupils are equal and reactive,' he said to Clare. He turned back to Simon. 'Do you have double vision or any blurring?'

'No,' he replied.

'Did you vomit?' Clare asked.

He shook his head, immediately regretting doing so. 'No, but I've got a cracking headache.'

'Were you in a car?' Fabian asked.

'Can't remember,' said Simon.

'Have you been drinking?' Fabian couldn't detect alcohol on his breath.

'No.'

Fabian turned to Clare. 'He might have slight concussion, don't you think? Especially as he's exhibiting pre-traumatic amnesia.'

'Who are you?' Simon asked him, as if noticing Fabian for the first time.

'This is Fabian, who's also a doctor,' said Clare, getting a clean cloth and bowl of water to attend to her brother's wounds. 'He's a colleague from the medical centre, so it's your lucky day—two doctors for the price of one.'

'I wouldn't call it a lucky day.' He studied Fabian for a few moments. 'What happened to Jason?'

'That's all over,' said Clare. 'Didn't Mum and Dad tell you?'

'I've been out of the country for a week or two,' said Simon. 'I was trying to get some money that was owed me.'

'Not those crooked time-share people you used to

work for?' said Clare, patting the damp cloth on his blood-covered face.

'Ouch!'

'Sorry, love, but I've got to get it clean. There might be glass in there if you've had a car accident.'

'Car accident?' said Simon. 'Who said anything about a car accident?'

'You did,' replied Fabian. Clare's brother definitely seemed to be acting in a very confused way. 'Did you lose consciousness at all?' he asked, concerned that perhaps the young man should have a skull X-ray in case there was a fracture.

'No.'

'You seem very sure about that and yet you couldn't remember whether you'd been in a car accident. I really think we should get you to hospital for observation and tests. You might have a fracture or a brain haemorrhage.'

Simon became agitated. 'No way! I'm not going into hospital because there's no need. I remember what happened perfectly—and it wasn't a car accident. It was some guys who beat me up.'

'Then we must call the police!' said Clare, shocked by the idea of her brother having been mugged. 'Did this happen in the street outside my flat?'

'Er, no,' said Simon. 'I came here by taxi. There's no point in getting the cops involved.'

This was beginning to sound very suspicious to Fabian.

'Why didn't you go straight to hospital instead of coming to Clare's flat? She might not have been in,' said Fabian.

'I took a chance on it,' said Simon. He shrugged his shoulders in a carefree way. 'I'm a bit of a gambler.

I'd rather let my sis patch me up than wait half the night in Casualty to be seen.'

'Quite right,' said Clare solicitously. 'I think I'm going to have to put a couple of stitches in this cut. And with all the bruising to your head you really need to have someone with you for the next few hours just in case you have suffered concussion.'

Simon grinned at her cheekily. 'I thought I could stay here, if that's all right with you?'

Fabian's heart sank into his boots. So much for their night of passion!

'If you don't need any more help from me, I'll be getting back home,' he said.

'Is that your Lotus parked outside?' Simon asked him.

'Yes, it is. Are you interested in sports cars?'

'I most certainly am. It's my new venture,' he said expansively.

'Another new venture?' said Clare.

She was finding it difficult to keep up with her brother's business career. The dodgy time-share enterprise was the last 'proper' job he'd had. Before that he'd gone through a succession of careers ranging from restaurant owner to ski instructor—with a marked lack of success in any of them. The failed restaurant venture had gobbled up most of the money he'd been left by his grandparents. Clare had invested her share of the inheritance in buying the flat she was now living in. She'd never dared say to Simon what a pity it was he hadn't bought himself a flat or house with the money instead of wasting it on a stupid restaurant that never had a cat in hell's chance of succeeding—but she'd been sorely tempted. The trouble was, she adored her brother. He might be a complete fool where money was concerned but he was such a captivating character—a man who could charm the birds off the trees—that she constantly found herself defending his feckless ways instead of criticising him. And now he was up to something else…another career, another venture!

'I'm buying and selling very specialist cars,' said Simon. 'That's why I noticed Fabian's Lotus.'

'You mean you're a second-hand car dealer?' said Clare, not even hiding her amusement. 'I think you may have at last found your *métier*, little brother.'

Simon winked at Fabian in a conspiratorial way. 'Women don't understand about cars, have you noticed that, Fabian? The cars that I'm talking about are specialist ones. Really great names—Lotus, Ferrari, Lamborghini—classic cars that will always be in demand by the discerning buyer. Cars that are a great investment as well as being a great way to pull the birds!'

'If you're not careful, I'll stitch your head without any local anaesthetic!' said Clare, smiling. She wasn't at all surprised at the way Simon was drawing Fabian into his sphere of influence. Men found him just as charming as women did.

'If you're interested in trading up from your Lotus I've got a terrific Ferrari that I could put your way,' said Simon. 'Beautiful condition, drives like a dream. Very reasonably priced.'

'I'll think about it,' said Fabian who was planning to do nothing of the kind. All he was thinking about as he left Clare's flat was how frustrated he was. 'I still think you should tell the police. Otherwise it could put Clare in a difficult position if there are any repercussions.'

Simon winked at him again. 'I'll think about it,' he said.

When Fabian had gone, Simon became more serious. 'You won't have to tell the police, will you?'

Clare was becoming increasingly worried about Simon's behaviour. First of all he'd said he'd been in a road accident, then he'd said he couldn't remember if he'd been in a car—and then he'd mentioned that he'd been beaten up by a gang of men. The last explanation would seem to be the most likely, given the type of injuries he'd suffered.

'I think you're hiding something,' she said. 'How can you expect me to give you my support if you're keeping something back? So, who were these guys that beat you up? Did you know them?'

'No,' Simon answered quickly but then, seeing the stern look in his sister's eyes, said, 'Yes.'

'Is that why you don't want the police to know about it?'

'Yes.' There was a long pause before he added, 'I'm scared they'll make things worse for me if I squeal.'

Clare was shocked at the implication of his last remark. 'It sounds to me as if you've got involved with a drugs gang.'

Simon sat bolt upright. 'What makes you say that?' His cheery attitude had definitely disappeared and he looked a very frightened man.

'You are, aren't you? You're either involved with drugs or money, or both. How could you be so stupid?' She was beginning to feel frightened herself.

Simon waved his hands in the air dismissively. 'It was all a terrible mistake. I'm not involved in drugs but somehow *they* thought I was. It all happened in Spain when I was trying to get the money I was owed.

Apparently these particular time-share dealers were involved in drugs...and somehow their contacts over here thought I was also involved.'

'But you're not?' Clare closed her eyes and crossed her fingers as she waited for him to reply.

'No, honestly I'm not.' Simon had put on his most appealing look, all liquid eyes and innocent smile.

She wanted to believe him. Simon was a fool in many ways but he wasn't evil. He wasn't the kind of person who became a drug dealer. At least, she hoped to heaven he wasn't.

Simon stayed for a couple of days. Clare had impressed on him how important it was to tell her if he had any symptoms of concussion. Thankfully, he seemed to be correct in his assertion that he didn't need to go to hospital. Clare suspected that he'd come to her place in order to lie low and keep out of the way of the drugs gang.

When he left on the third day he assured her that everything was going to be fine. He'd been in touch by phone with his contact in Spain and was convinced that the message would get through to the gang in England that he was not a drugs courier and was therefore of no further interest to them.

'Promise me you'll keep away from dodgy people in future,' said Clare, though realising it was a futile thing to ask of her brother.

'Sure. You can trust me, sis.' At the door he turned to her. 'Don't tell your friend Fabian about the drugs connection, will you? Or Mum or Dad. I want to forget all about it.'

'OK,' said Clare, hoping against hope that this time he *had* turned a new page.

*   *   *

A few days later, Fabian invited Clare out to an expensive restaurant.

'You deserve a treat,' he told her, 'after playing nursemaid to your kid brother.'

Clare spent longer than usual getting ready to go out. Even though she was going out with a man she saw virtually every working day, she still wanted to make herself look special for tonight.

When Fabian called to pick her up she was conscious of the way his eyes focused on her willowy body, travelling from the swell of her breasts beneath the sapphire silk of the dress to its short, above-the-knee skirt which fell in flattering folds around her long, smooth, bare legs.

'You look beautiful,' he said huskily, slipping an arm protectively around her as he led her to his car.

'Thanks,' she said. 'You don't look too bad yourself.' He did indeed look stunningly handsome, she thought, in a light grey suit and pale blue shirt.

The excellence of the dinner and the ambience in the restaurant made the evening a memorable occasion. It was so romantic that often, during a lull in their conversation, they would just gaze into each other's eyes. The gaps in conversation lengthened and, for what seemed an age, they sat just holding hands, hardly noticing that their coffee had gone stone cold in the meantime.

'Are you ready to go home?' he asked, his voice soft and caressing.

'Yes,' she replied. She felt a deep aching in the centre of her body as she experienced a hunger which only he could satisfy.

They drove in silence to her flat. The first words he spoke when she turned the key in the lock were, 'If anyone rings your doorbell tonight, you're definitely not going to answer it. And that's an order.'

'Yes, Doctor,' she said, kicking off her high heels and letting him pull her into his arms.

He towered over her as he gathered her to him, pressing his hard, powerful body against the softness of hers. Her arms went around his neck and her whole body tilted against him as he kissed her. Her lips parted in fevered response.

'Oh, Clare,' he muttered thickly, moving his hands seductively down her back, following the sensual curves of her body beneath the thin silk of her dress.

They undressed quickly—as quickly as they could in their desperate need for each other.

'I'm burning for you,' he said, scooping her in his arms and lifting her onto the bed.

The fire of passion licked through them both. He devoured her with his lips while his hands touched her in all the right places, so that by the time he entered her she was almost screaming for him in a frenzy of desire.

Afterwards, as they lay satiated in each other's arms, he nuzzled his face to hers. 'I love you,' he said. 'I don't know if I mentioned it before.'

Her heart skipped a beat as he said the words she'd longed to hear him say. She was supremely happy and couldn't imagine anyone in the world being as happy as she was at that particular moment. 'I love you, too,' she whispered, before drifting off to sleep in her lover's arms.

Back at The Hawthorns the following day, Clare was finding it hard to concentrate on work after the previous night.

'Mrs Sandra Dorlish, Room Three please,' she said

into the intercom. After a few moments a sandy-haired middle-aged woman walked in.

'Good morning, Doctor,' she said as she sat down on the chair opposite Clare.

'What can I do for you, Mrs Dorlish?' Clare asked after casting her eyes over the computer screen. 'No problems with the HRT?'

'No, that's fine,' Sandra replied. Then she rolled up her sleeve. 'It's this mole on my arm. I'm sure it's nothing to worry about but you hear such awful stories about skin cancer and everything.'

Clare rose and went over to the patient to get a closer look at the flat brown mark that was the cause of concern.

'Has it changed in size or shape recently?' Clare asked.

'It's got a little bigger and that was what worried me. Then I banged it on a cupboard and made it bleed and that worried me even more.'

'Does it itch?'

'No.'

Clare then scrutinised the mole, looking closely at it with a magnifying glass. 'The bleeding seems to have come from a small cut next to the mole, not the mole itself.'

'That's a relief,' Sandra said, rolling down her shirt-sleeve. 'So I don't need to put any cream or anything on it?'

Clare went back to her desk. 'The best thing is just to leave it—but of course keep checking on it from time to time and if it changes in shape or size, or if it becomes itchy or bleeds, come back to see me again.'

Sandra buttoned her sleeve. 'I've been worried about something else, actually.'

Clare looked at her encouragingly. 'Well, now's the time to tell me if you've any other problems.'

'It's not about me,' Sandra said. 'It's my daughter, Sally. She's been getting some very high temperatures lately—I mean *really* high. But the next day she will be back to normal. She insists there's nothing wrong with her and calls me a fusspot when I say she should come and see one of the doctors.'

Clare tapped Sally Dorlish's name into the computer and brought up her file.

'Your daughter's nineteen, is that right?' Clare asked.

'Yes. She's just completed a very exciting gap year as a volunteer in India before starting university. I did wonder if it was glandular fever and whether she should have a blood test for that.'

'She spent her gap year in India?' Clare queried. 'I wonder if she could be suffering from malaria?'

'Definitely not,' Sandra said emphatically. 'Sally was working as a medical assistant handing out anti-malarial drugs to everyone concerned. She made darned sure that she took the full course herself. No, I'd say that malaria is the one thing you can rule out. She says it's just a bout of flu—but it's gone on for weeks now and her dad and I are getting really worried.'

Clare searched in her desk for a blood-test request form. She filled in Sally's details and handed the form to Sandra.

'From what you say I think Sally should have a blood test—and we can check for glandular fever at the same time. The path lab at St Margaret's is open every day and the results will be sent through to me.'

Sandra took the form. 'Thanks, Doctor. I'll try and persuade her to get the test done—but she's a very

independent-minded young woman and won't do anything she doesn't want to.'

'I've never met her,' Clare said, 'but she sounds a
very caring person, working as a volunteer in India.'

Clare did meet Sally Dorlish—and sooner than she
thought. Later that day, at the close of evening surgery,
she received a frantic phone call from Sandra.

'I'm so worried about Sally. I've just taken her temperature and it's one hundred and five! And she's shaking like a leaf—saying she's icy cold.'

'I'll be over there in a few minutes,' Clare said.

On arrival at the Dorlishes' house, Clare was taken
straight to the bedside of the sick girl.

'I feel so cold,' Sally said through chattering teeth.

'We've given her a warm bath,' her mother said, 'but
it made no difference. And then I wondered if I should
have made it a cold bath to try and bring her temperature down. But she was shivering so much.' Sandra's
face was grey with anxiety.

Clare took the girl's temperature and confirmed that
it was very high. Her blood pressure, on the other hand,
was very low.

'I'm calling for an ambulance,' Clare said. 'And to
be on the safe side, with Sally having so recently been
in India, I'm going to suggest they put her in an isolation ward.'

'Oh, no,' said Sandra. 'What do you think it is? Yel-
low fever or green monkey disease or something dreadful like that?'

Clare shook her head. 'No, but I think it could be
malaria.'

'That's impossible! She took all the pills, had all the
right drugs. She couldn't possibly have malaria!'

'I'm afraid the antimalarial drugs are not one hundred per cent effective in every case. Sally could be in that unlucky minority of people who get the disease even though they've taken every precaution.'

At the next practice meeting, Brian brought up the subject of Sally Dorlish.

'Congratulations on the diagnosis,' he said. 'The girl was very unlucky to have picked up that particular strain of malaria—*Plasmodium vivax*—because the routinely used malarial drugs are not particularly effective in preventing vivax.'

Fabian glanced across at Clare. 'Sally was lucky in one respect. She was lucky that Clare recognised that it was probably malaria…after all, it's not the kind of illness we come across too often in The Hawthorns.'

'Just wait for global warming,' said Sam.

Two weeks later, Fabian popped his head around her door at the medical centre, checking that she was alone.

She was grabbing a quick lunch, having a sandwich at her desk.

'Come in,' she said gesturing to him.

'How do you fancy a few days in Florida, leaving next week?' he asked.

She leaned back in her chair and stretched languorously. 'That sounds just the right kind of medicine for me. I haven't had a holiday in ages.'

'Good. In that case, I'll book the flights. It's short notice but I've checked with Sam and Brian and they're happy to let us go. There's a good locum who can cover for us and it's a good time of year to be away…no epidemics on the horizon that I know of.'

She gently pulled on his tie, bringing his face close to hers so that she could kiss him.

'You're a miracle-worker, that's what you are. What

brought all this on? You've never mentioned Florida before.'

'It's going to be a little more than a holiday,' Fabian admitted. 'I'm doing some sleuthing. I'm going to try and find out more about my real father, this George Merrick. My mother's given me the address—on condition that I don't do anything to upset his family who don't know about my existence.'

Clare took a sip of her orange juice. 'What kind of family does he have, do you know?'

'A wife, or should I say, widow. And four grown-up children.' Fabian paused. 'I'm not interested in giving them the kind of shock I received when I learned that he was my father.'

Clare pondered this. 'I wouldn't worry too much about that. It couldn't possibly be anything like the horrendous shock that you got on learning the truth. His widow wouldn't be too happy to know that her late hubby had a secret child, but her children might find it very interesting to discover that they have a half-sibling.'

'I guess I'll play it by ear,' said Fabian, 'and see what happens when I get there. But primarily I'd just like to go to where George lived and get a feel for the place. It would help me to come to terms with who I am by learning a little about who he was.'

'Any excuse for a holiday in Florida, say I.' Clare smiled at him before turning to her desk diary. 'What dates do you have in mind?'

CHAPTER FIVE

FABIAN drove the hired car from Orlando airport and, with Clare navigating, was relieved to find they'd correctly negotiated the web-like mass of intersections and were finally on Interstate 4 going west.

'Isn't this fun?' exclaimed Clare when they could relax and enjoy the drive through the heart of Florida to their destination on the west coast.

They ignored all the tempting signs to Disney World and other theme parks. Clare expressed her disappointment.

'We haven't time to do all that,' said Fabian who was single-mindedly focused on heading for the Sarasota area and the address given to him by his mother. He touched her hand. 'You need to have children to go to places like that,' he said. 'We'll come here again when we've got some.'

'Do you mean you want to borrow some? Or were you planning on having some of your own?'

'I don't believe in borrowing anything,' he said, stroking his hand over hers again.

A comforting warmth spread throughout her relaxed body. It was the first time Fabian had mentioned the possibility of having children. Up until that moment she'd been acutely aware of his negative attitude towards fatherhood—largely, she suspected, because of his own unhappy childhood.

They spent their first night in Florida in a motel off

Highway 41. The kingsize bed, one of two in the room, was the largest she had ever seen let alone slept in.

After their first all-American breakfast which included, at Clare's insistence, pancakes, bacon and maple syrup, they set off towards their destination. For the last leg of their journey they took a scenic route, through Bradenton and Anna Maria Island, following a chain of barrier islands until they reached the Sarasota County boundary.

'We've arrived,' said Fabian as they approached a pretty town rising on a gentle hillside beside the blue waters of Sarasota Bay.

'This looks a wealthy area—even by Florida standards,' remarked Clare as they drove through the outskirts of town with its abundance of well-tended houses and manicured lawns.

'It's a strange feeling now that we've arrived at the place where my real father lived and worked for many years of his life.'

Before looking up the address his mother had given him, they drove around hoping to find somewhere suitable to stay for a night or two. On one of the boulevards they found the ideal place, a small inn close to beautiful tropical gardens and overlooking a marina. After they'd checked in and taken a shower to freshen up, Clare could sense that Fabian was extremely keen on setting about finding his roots. At Reception they'd been given a town map showing the streets and suburbs in greater detail than the road map they'd been using.

'I've found it!' said Fabian after studying the map for several minutes. 'It's not far from the centre of town.'

The man on Reception struck up a conversation

when he heard Clare and Fabian chatting to each other on their way out.

'You folks going to see the Ringling Museum?' he asked. 'He's the guy who made millions with his circus. He bought a great mansion and filled it with European art and treasures. I thought with you being British you'd be interested.'

'I'm sure we'll go there soon,' said Fabian, returning the friendly smile. 'And the car museum, too.'

'Have a nice day,' said the man, admiring the sexy back view of the young lady in the split denim skirt.

Following their new map, they drove along the attractive waterfront, past stylish shops and tropical gardens and out towards a housing development a few miles from the centre of town. Turning down a shady, tree-lined avenue Fabian stopped the car outside one of the large detached houses and switched off the engine.

'This is it,' he said, staring out of the driver's window. 'This is where my father lived.'

They both sat in awed silence for a few minutes as Fabian took in all the details of the house and garden. He was just about to reach for his camera to take a photograph of the house when a woman drove into the driveway and parked in front of the garage doors. Fabian quickly put away his camera when he saw that the woman was looking directly at him as she got out of the driver's seat.

'Do you think that's George Merrick's widow?' asked Clare in a hushed voice.

Before Fabian was able to reply the woman, carrying a bag of groceries, had walked over to them.

'Can I help you?' she asked, having noticed the

strange car parked outside her house. 'Are you looking
for someone?'

Throwing caution to the wind, he replied, 'Yes, I'm
looking for a Mrs Merrick.'

'That's me,' she said. 'Why do you want to see me?'
She paused for a split second before adding, 'You're
British, aren't you? I don't get to speak to many British
people…it's so nice to hear your accent.'

Fabian turned quickly to Clare, giving her a warning
look. 'I'm not going to tell her,' he murmured between
clenched teeth. He opened his car door and stepped
onto the pavement. 'Actually, I'm wondering if I've
got the right Mrs Merrick. Is there another Mrs Merrick
who lives near here?' Fabian was speaking off the top
of his head. What he didn't want to do was to announce
to this sweet-faced middle-aged woman that he was her
late husband's love-child.

'Do you mean Sylvia?' she asked unsuspectingly.
'She's married to my son Brad.'

'Yes, that's who I'm looking for,' said Fabian, making a mental note of the names. 'I'll look them up in
the phone book. I'm terribly sorry to have bothered
you, Mrs Merrick.'

'If you just wait a minute I'll jot down their address
for you. It's only a couple of miles from here.' She
attempted to juggle the shopping bag from one arm to
the other and nearly dropped it.

'Let me carry that,' said Fabian, taking the bag from
her and following her to the step. She took a notepad
from her shoulder-bag, scribbled an address and phone
number down, tore off the sheet and handed it to him.
'There you are, Mr…?'

'Drumm,' said Fabian, taking the proffered sheet of
paper. 'And thank you so much.'

He returned to the car and waving to Mrs Merrick drove quickly away.

'You bottled out, didn't you?' said Clare.

'I couldn't bring myself to tell her. So I reverted to Plan B which is to contact one of the four children and hope my courage doesn't run out again.'

Clare leaned over and kissed him on the cheek. 'That's the trouble with being such a sensitive creature. But I love you for it.'

A short time later they were parked outside another house. Clare remained in the car as before and Fabian got out and walked to the front door. There were children's toys scattered around the garden and, as he stood at the door ringing the bell, a couple of boys aged about eight appeared from around the side of the house.

'Do you want Mom?' one of them asked. 'She's in the bathroom at the moment.'

'I've come to speak to Mrs Merrick,' said Fabian. 'Or Mr Merrick.'

'Dad's gone fishing and so it'll have to be Mom,' said the other boy. Fabian wondered if they were twins because although they weren't identical they were definitely very close in age. As he was thinking these thoughts, he heard the sound of a cistern being flushed and footsteps from inside the house. The door opened and a blonde woman of a similar age to himself stood there.

'He's looking for you, Mom,' said the first boy, 'but I told him you were in the bathroom.'

The woman looked embarrassed at the notion of her children discussing such things with a perfect stranger. 'Put your games away,' she said quickly covering up their gaffe, 'if you want to go to the beach.'

The two boys disappeared round the back of the house from where they'd come.

'Mrs Sylvia Merrick?' asked Fabian.

'Yes.'

'My name's Fabian Drumm. I live in England. You don't know me but I think I might be related to your husband.'

'Oh,' she said, 'like a distant cousin or something? And you've come all the way from England to find us?' She seemed quite taken with the idea. She was an only child herself with no cousins or close relatives apart from her parents. Her husband Brad was one of four children and that was an added attraction to marrying him…all the extra family members he brought with him, so to speak. And now here was this handsome stranger with a cute British accent standing on her doorstep.

'Yes, something like a distant cousin,' said Fabian. 'Perhaps I should come back later when your husband is home?'

'That's probably the best idea,' she said, glancing at her watch. 'I promised to take the boys to the beach and we need to be setting off soon. You know what kids are like when you've made a promise!' She looked past him to where Clare was waiting in the car. 'I hope your wife doesn't think I'm rude not asking you both in…'

'That's no problem,' said Fabian. 'What time shall we come back?'

'About six-thirty—is that OK with you? Brad will be sure to be home by then.' She smiled broadly, revealing a large expanse of dazzling white teeth.

Fabian and Clare spent the day exploring the extremely pleasant downtown area of Sarasota, browsing around the many excellent bookshops before lunching in a good restaurant and wandering down to the quayside waterfront.

In the afternoon they visited the Ringling Museum, as suggested by the hotel desk clerk. The large complex of buildings and grounds had been given to the state of Florida by the circus entrepreneur John Ringling. There were so many magnificent treasures to be seen that Fabian and Clare felt they were in danger of cultural overload. They did make time, however, to call in to the nearby car museum which housed more than a hundred old cars. Fabian found himself drooling over a 1954 Packard.

'That is fabulous,' he said admiringly.

'I bet Simon could get you one of those, for a price,' said Clare.

'I very much doubt that your brother would ever come across anything like this,' said Fabian. 'This one is so rare. It's not just an old car…' He stopped in mid-sentence when he saw Clare's expression.

'I was joking,' she said, reaching up and giving him a kiss. 'Haven't we seen enough old cars for one day? How about a siesta back at the hotel?'

'It's a bit late for a siesta, but I'm in favour of the general principle,' he said huskily, putting an arm round her and kissing her on the mouth.

At half past six, Fabian parked their car outside Sylvia and Brad's house and switched off the engine.

'Are you sure you want me to come in with you?' Clare asked. 'Wouldn't it be better if I stayed out here until you've broken the news to Brad? It isn't really any of my business and you might want to be alone when you…'

He pulled her gently to him, kissing her on the cheek. 'I want you there,' he said. 'It *is* your business—or at least I *want* it to be your business because I love you. I want to share everything with you, even something as emotionally important as this.' He kissed her on the lips.

'We'd better go in,' she said, her blue eyes sparkling. 'Otherwise they'll think we're going to spend the evening parked outside their house snogging in the car.'

Clare had spoken flippantly but deep inside she was feeling very emotional and close to crying tears of happiness. Fabian had told her, in no uncertain terms, that he loved her and wanted to share everything in his life with her.

'Snogging, eh? Stop putting ideas into my head, woman,' he said, pulling away reluctantly and getting out of the car.

As they walked up the path, the front door was opened by Sylvia. She gave them her dazzling white smile but it didn't reach her eyes. There was a hard edge to her voice as she said, 'Hi there. I was speaking to Brad's mother after you left earlier today. She said you'd been round to her house earlier. So, Mr Drumm, if you are a distant cousin why didn't you mention this to her?' The smile was still hovering on her lips but it had become more fixed.

'It's Dr Drumm, actually,' said Fabian playing for time. 'And this is Dr Clare Westwood. It's true I didn't say anything to your mother-in-law about being related…but I can explain all about it.'

As he was speaking he looked over Sylvia's shoulder and saw the figure of a man approaching.

'Hi,' he said. 'I'm Brad.' He stood next to his wife.

'We've kinda learned to be suspicious of strangers of late,' Sylvia said, still hesitating about asking them into the house.

There was a short silence as all four stared at each other—then Clare gave a small gasp. Everyone looked at her.

'What's the matter?' Fabian asked under his breath.

'I'm sorry,' said Clare, 'but I just…I just can't get over how alike you two men are.'

Fabian, who hadn't been paying much attention to those kind of details, turned to look at Brad and to study him more closely. He was a man of similar height to himself, with the same dark brown hair and distinctive shape of nose. He found it hard to decide in that split second whether or not there was more than a passing resemblance but Sylvia had certainly noticed it.

'Oh, Lord,' she gasped, 'I see what you mean. You are *very* alike. Now why didn't I notice that before? It must have been the British accent that distracted me.'

'Let me explain,' said Fabian. 'I didn't mention anything to Mrs Merrick because I wasn't sure how she'd take the news about me being a relative of her husband's…one that she didn't know existed. I thought the news might be better coming from you.'

'Come in,' said Brad. 'You look pretty genuine to me. In fact you look the spitting image of my sister, Bonnie.'

Sylvia stood back to let them in. 'Poor Bonnie,' she said quietly as they walked into the hallway.

'Why do you say "poor Bonnie"?' Fabian enquired. He noticed the way Brad threw a warning glance in

Sylvia's direction. He interpreted it as a signal to keep quiet.

'I'm afraid Bonnie isn't well,' said Brad. 'She's in a special place.'

The curtness with which he imparted this information meant, for the time being at least, that the subject was closed. A chill ran through Fabian's body. Just as he found out he had a half-sister who was his spitting image, he also discovered that she had some sort of problem. Whether the problem was mental or physical was not made clear and he could only speculate.

They went through into a large, airy room which looked out onto a small back garden. The TV was on in one corner of the room and both boys were watching cartoons.

'This is Lewis and Brad Junior,' said Sylvia. 'Say hi to…Fabian and Clare, wasn't it?'

'That's right,' said Fabian. 'Hi, Brad and Lewis.'

'Hi,' said Clare, smiling encouragingly at them.

'Hi,' they replied in unison, moving their heads slightly but keeping their eyes fixed on the TV screen.

The four adults sat down on the comfy, brightly coloured soft furniture.

'Are they twins?' Clare asked. 'They seem very close in age.'

'They're both eight years old,' replied Sylvia, 'but they're not twins. We adopted them.'

'That's nice,' said Clare effusively. 'It must have been difficult finding you couldn't have children, especially as you so obviously wanted them. You were lucky in getting two such lovely boys.' She realised she was gushing like this because she was nervous. She hoped it didn't come across as being too intrusive about what was obviously a very personal matter, especially as she noted that Sylvia's smile was no longer fixed on her lips.

'Yes, we are lucky,' said Sylvia. 'We adopted them at around two years old after we'd decided not to have children of our own.'

It was a strange remark to make, thought Clare, but she decided not to pursue it any further as there were possibly very good, and private, reasons for her saying it. It might be that Sylvia and Brad were unable to have children but were unwilling to openly admit to one of them being infertile and wanted to make it sound as if they adopted their children as a matter of choice rather than necessity. She was glad when Brad changed the subject.

'Tell us about these British cousins we didn't know about,' said Brad.

Fabian cast a swift glance across the room. The boys were engrossed in their TV programme. Nevertheless, when he spoke it was in a low voice.

'I'm not a cousin of yours,' he said. 'I'm your half-brother.'

'Half-brother?' exclaimed Brad in disbelief. 'How can that be? Mom never said anything about that.'

'She doesn't know about me. In fact, I only discovered the truth a few weeks ago when I'd been left a legacy by your father.'

Brad took this information in slowly. He narrowed his eyes. 'What did you say your name was again?'

'Drumm. Dr Fabian Drumm.'

'That explains it,' he said. 'I read that name in the will, but I just assumed it was a donation to some sort of medical institute. Somewhere in Paris, wasn't it?'

Fabian nodded. 'That's where my mother lives.'

Brad paused while he took in this extra piece of in-

formation. 'My father left dozens of legacies and do-
nations and all that sort of thing. He was a wealthy
man and wanted to put something back into society.
Della and I hadn't gotten round to sorting everything
out. We left all that to the lawyers.'

'Della?' queried Fabian.

'She's my other sister,' replied Brad. 'I tell you
what... I'll go through my family and you can fill us
in on yours. I'm one of four children. My eldest sister
is Bonnie, she's forty-five, Della is forty-two, my
brother Glen is forty and I'm thirty-eight.'

'I'm thirty-two,' replied Fabian, 'and I'm an only
child. My mother is French and I'd always believed
that my father was the Englishman to whom she was
married. But I've recently learned that your father was
my real father. He was working in Paris at the time—
and he and my mother had a brief affair which resulted
in my conception. Your father wanted to return to
America to his wife and children and that's what he
did. Working it out, I now see that you would have all
been very young at the time. I presume he never told
your mother—but I can't be sure of that. All I know is
that when I met her yesterday I couldn't bring myself
to tell her that I was her husband's child. There's no
point in causing unnecessary pain, is there?'

Sylvia and Brad remained silent, taking in this sur-
prising news.

'No,' said Brad after a pause. 'We'd better not tell
her just yet. She's had more than her fair share of pain
and trouble.'

'That's what I thought,' said Fabian. 'She's only recently been widowed and must be feeling very vulnerable right now.'

They continued chatting. Brad and Fabian, in partic-

ular, were each fascinated by the details of a life previously unknown to the other. They learned that Della
lived outside Tampa with her husband and three children. Glen was married but had no children. He worked
with Brad, running their father's construction business.
No further mention was made of Bonnie.

Brad and Sylvia were fascinated to learn about
Fabian's French mother and cross-examined him in
great detail about Paris, hinting that they were planning
on visiting Europe in the near future. They were also
keen to learn about Clare's relatives in Ireland as well
as hearing about The Hawthorns medical centre. Sylvia
had picked up a notepad and was writing down all the
contact numbers and address details that Fabian and
Clare mentioned. It was obvious that Fabian was going
to be seeing a whole lot more of his new-found
American family in the not-too-distant future.

Over supper—delicious pizzas that Sylvia had dug
out of the freezer, served with a crisp salad and Brad's
home-made dressing—everyone seemed relaxed and
happy and they chatted as if they'd known each other
all their lives. Sylvia kept probing to try and find out
if Fabian and Clare were contemplating marriage, and
from Fabian's responses it was clear to everyone that
he most definitely *was*…but he had no intention of being bounced into a public proposal by Sylvia.

'Where are you staying?' Brad asked them.

They mentioned the name of their hotel.

'That's a good place,' he said, 'but if you'd like to
have a few days by the ocean we have a family holiday
home on one of the barrier islands. It's fully equipped
with linens and kitchen stuff and food in the freezer.
There's nobody using it at the moment and you're very

welcome to spend a few days there, relaxing and soaking up the Florida sun.'

Fabian and Clare were delighted with the idea, especially when Sylvia brought out photographs of the house, set in grounds which ran down to a beach.

'There's also a little motorboat,' said Brad, showing them a picture of a sleek speedboat with an outboard motor.

They arranged to stay three days at the Merricks' beach house, starting the following day.

'It really is so kind of you,' said Clare, overcome by the generosity of these two people who had been complete strangers until a few hours ago.

'You're very trusting,' said Fabian, wondering if he would have been quite so generous in similar circumstances. 'I'll give you references from England and France if you want to check up on us before finally deciding.'

Brad waved his hands dismissively. 'I've got a well-developed instinct for rooting out bogus people,' he said. 'I've been in business long enough to know who to trust and who not to trust. You seem genuine to me—and, damn it, you look like a Merrick even though your name's Drumm!' He grasped Fabian by the hand. 'You're my half-brother...I don't need a DNA test to tell me that!'

Even so, Fabian was amused to see that Brad picked up the piece of paper with the names and phone numbers and, folding it in half, slipped it into his shirt pocket. A successful businessman like Brad would never take any unnecessary risk and Fabian was certain that he'd be making a few discreet enquiries about him before the keys were handed over.

*   *   *

Back at the hotel, Fabian gathered Clare into his arms the moment he'd shut the door of their room. He held her tightly against him as if he would never let her go. His cheek rubbed against her hair and he murmured softly in her ear the words she had longed to hear him say.

'Will you marry me?' His voice was low and husky but his words rang loud and clear as far as Clare was concerned.

'Yes,' she replied, her voice almost a whisper.

His whole body seemed to relax and he enveloped her in a bear hug. Then he held her away and looked deep into her eyes.

'You don't mind then?'

'What?'

'Not having the romantic setting of the Eiffel Tower for my proposal? I know how much it would have meant to you. I had planned to take you to Paris again and do just that...but I was impatient to know your answer.'

There was a touching sincerity in his voice and a nervousness that moved Clare deeply. Did he really think she would have turned him down?

'I think Florida is a very romantic place for a proposal,' she said, snuggling her head into his chest. 'Just as romantic as the Eiffel Tower.'

'It will always be a special place for me,' said Fabian, stroking her hair and turning her face to his. 'At last I know who I am and that knowledge has set me free from the past.'

She lifted her head until their mouths were touching. 'I've always known who you were,' she said. 'You're the man I love.'

'Oh, my darling,' he muttered against her lips. 'I

never thought I'd ever be able to commit myself to marriage and now I can't wait for…'

His words were lost as they kissed hungrily, lighting the fires of their passion once more.

The Merricks' beach house was wonderful and every bit as attractive as it had appeared in the photographs. It was on a superb sandy beach facing the Gulf of Mexico and was, Brad assured them, in one of the quieter, more peaceful areas in the very popular resort.

For two days they were left on their own to enjoy the sun and sea and the sanctuary of the beautiful holiday home. They spent happy days swimming and lazing around, going for trips in the speedboat and helping themselves to food from the well-stocked freezer ('I insist that you do,' instructed Sylvia). The nights were as romantic as anything Clare could ever have envisaged. Her only regret was that this wasn't their honeymoon because she found herself wondering where on earth they could possibly go that would match up to this.

On their third and final day, Brad and Sylvia arranged for several other members of the Merrick family to join them for a get-together. Glen came along, as did his sister Della and two of her three children. Brad hadn't yet broken the news to his mother and would wait until Fabian and Clare had left for England before broaching the subject, he told them.

All ten went out for lunch at a favourite beach restaurant. Fabian insisted on paying.

'Please, Brad,' he said firmly when his half-brother waved his credit card at the waiter. 'It'll make me feel so much better about accepting your hospitality if you let me pay for this.'

'Well, if you insist,' said Brad genially. 'But you'll get plenty of chance to repay the hospitality when we come over to Europe.'

'It will be my pleasure,' said Fabian. 'And my mother will be delighted, I know, to put you up in Paris. I'll persuade her to come and visit me in England for a week or so and then you can have the whole place to yourself.'

'Clare tells me you are planning on getting married soon,' he said as he accompanied Fabian to the bar so that he could sign the credit-card slip.

'That's right,' he confirmed. 'It must have been the romantic Florida atmosphere that did it…finally pushed me into proposing.' He wasn't going to start explaining why, in the past, he'd had a mental block about marriage and children.

Fabian signed the credit-card slip having first added a generous tip. As the two men were walking back to the table, Brad put a hand on Fabian's arm and stopped him from joining the others immediately.

'There's something I have to tell you,' he said. His face was sombre. A nervous tic flickered by the side of one eye.

'I think I know what you're going to say,' said Fabian. 'It's about Bonnie, isn't it? Her name hasn't been mentioned since the first day we met.'

Brad looked down at his feet as if unable to meet Fabian's gaze.

'That's right. But I can't tell you here. If we let the others go back to the house, we'll make some excuse for driving to the store to buy something. I need to tell you quietly and alone. It's not something that can be rushed—but it's something I have to tell you. It's desperately important that I do.'

*   *   *

Later that evening, after they'd waved goodbye to the various members of the Merrick clan, Clare went up to Fabian and put an arm round his waist.

'You've gone quiet,' she said, planting a kiss on his warm cheek. 'Were you a little overwhelmed by your big new family? Now you know what it's like in the Westwood household at Christmas—dozens of relatives from all over the place! But I love it.' She kissed him again. 'Not as much as I love you, of course.'

She kissed him once more and when she realised that she wasn't getting any response she dropped her arm away from him.

'What's the matter?' she asked. 'Do you feel ill?' He'd certainly gone a lot paler than usual.

He stiffened slightly. 'Nothing's the matter. I'm not ill. I feel fine. Just a little tired, perhaps.'

She put both arms around him this time, cuddling him gently. 'I know a great way to make you feel wide awake and not at all tired. It's our last night in this blissful place so we'd better not waste it. How about early to bed?' She rubbed herself up against him seductively.

He responded by taking her hands from him and stepping back.

'I think I *will* go to bed early,' he said, his voice flat. 'We've got a long drive ahead of us tomorrow.'

She was stunned by his change of mood. It was as if she was sharing the beach house with a different man. Her loving, sexy, caring man had turned into a cold fish.

She gave a sigh as she watched his retreating back. Was this just one of his moods? Did he often behave in such an irrational way for no explicable reason?

There was so much she didn't know or understand about him—this man she'd agreed to marry.

Following him into the bedroom she decided not to say anything that might make his mood worse. She undressed, slid under the duvet and positioned herself next to him, their bodies barely touching. Previously, Fabian would have moved closer to her, wrapping his naked limbs around hers as a prelude to making love. It took hardly a touch from her to make desire flare up in him—and she'd loved the way he never seemed to tire of her, his appetite insatiable, his body always ready for love.

Tonight, however, he turned his back and moved to the far side of the bed.

He must be sick! said Clare to herself, deciding that tomorrow would be better. Tomorrow he would be rid of whatever it was that ailed him. She hoped.

CHAPTER SIX

ALL the way back to Orlando airport, Fabian's mood stayed the same. As they drove across Florida, Clare attempted to make light-hearted conversation but Fabian remained quiet and preoccupied. Then, out of the blue, his mood changed and he smiled at her for the first time that day. But it was a smile that had no warmth.

'Do you think there's the slightest chance you might be pregnant?' he asked after they'd stopped for petrol.

His question took her completely off guard.

'I'm not sure,' she said. Then, after giving it more thought, added, 'It's most unlikely. As you know, I'm on the Pill, but these things do happen—nothing's one hundred per cent guaranteed.'

'When will you know?' he asked, a nagging persistence entering his voice.

'In ten days' time,' she replied, 'but does it matter? We're getting married and I would imagine we'd hope to have children at some time in the future. If they come sooner rather than later, then so be it.'

She snuggled up to him, happy that he appeared to be coming out of his gloominess. But what he said next sent a chill through her.

'I'm not sure that I do want children,' he replied, starting the engine and heading for the highway.

Clare was open-mouthed.

'That's not what you said earlier!' she protested. 'You said you wanted children to take to Disney

World. At least that's what I *thought* you meant. Don't you remember, I asked you if you wanted to borrow some children and you said you didn't believe in borrowing anything?'

She turned to face him but he was looking straight ahead at the road. He said nothing.

'Don't you remember saying that?' she persisted.

Fabian shrugged.

'Lord, you can be so infuriating!' She switched on the car radio, roughly punching the buttons until she found a station with some suitably loud music to match her furious mood. But after ten minutes she switched it off again.

'This is important, you know!' she said between clenched teeth. 'It's a very important part of a relationship to me. I love children... I love babies. If we're going to get married I have to know if you want to have children or not.'

'I've just told you,' he said, his voice level and calm, 'that I'm not sure about wanting children. In fact I'll put it even more clearly, I *am* sure about it. Absolutely certain. I don't want any.'

Clare began to feel sick. How could she have been so wrong about Fabian? She'd believed they were soulmates, with the same values in life. She couldn't imagine marrying anyone who didn't want children. Of course, not being *able* to have children was a different matter. There was always the possibility that for some reason or other they never *would* have children of their own. As she said earlier—nothing was one hundred per cent guaranteed. But to set out right from the start *not* to have a family went totally against her nature.

For several miles she was silent—speechless, really. She just didn't know how to handle the situation. There was no point in getting hysterical and having a blazing row—that would achieve nothing, except perhaps a road accident.

At the airport they checked in their bags and waited for their flight to be called. There was definitely a frosty atmosphere between the two of them.

'Do you want a magazine to read on the flight?' Fabian asked formally.

'No,' she said, with equal coolness.

On the long flight home they watched movie after movie, headphones clamped on, isolating them from each other even though they were in adjoining seats.

An hour before they were due to land, Clare decided to grab the bull by the horns and broach the subject of babies in one final attempt at changing his mind.

'You might feel differently about children if they were your own,' she ventured.

'No,' he said firmly. 'I'm sorry, Clare, but that's how I am. Nothing will change my mind. I now realise that we should have talked the subject over before we got so in—'

'So in love?'

'So involved. You can't help who you fall in love with but you can decide who you want to spend your life with. Having or not having children is an important lifestyle decision and we should have talked about it before we decided to marry.'

'You think I'm still going to marry you, do you?'

'Aren't you?' He turned to her and she could see the pain and disappointment in his eyes.

She bit her lip. What a decision to have to make— in the early hours of the morning over the Atlantic Ocean!

'Can we go back to how we were before we agreed

to get married?' she asked tentatively. 'I still love you desperately and want to be with you…but you've turned out to be a different person from the man I said I'd marry.'

He reached out and held her hand, grasping it tightly in his. 'Let's do that,' he said, his voice thick with emotion.

As the plane approached the runway, Clare, who always crossed her fingers for a safe landing, also kept them crossed in the hope that this month against all the odds her contraceptive pills had failed. If she'd already become pregnant, then Fabian would have no choice in the matter. She would have his baby regardless of what he'd say. And she was sure he'd come round to the idea of fatherhood in a very short time once he held his own child in his arms.

Ten days later Clare got her period—and with it vanished all her hopes of having Fabian's baby. It depressed her greatly and for several days she found herself wiping away tears of sadness for what might have been.

She was kept very busy at the medical centre doing extra shifts for Brian who had taken a few days' holiday. One of her shifts was over at St Margaret's Hospital where she was helping out at a paediatric clinic, giving jabs and inoculations. During a break she went to the hospital staff canteen for a cup of tea and a chocolate biscuit.

Over in one corner of the canteen, a group of paramedics was gathered round one of their fellow workers. Someone was making a speech—Clare caught the odd word and realised it was some sort of leaving presentation. Her eyes roved around the room without focusing on anything in particular.

She'd enjoyed the morning clinic with the babies and young children…but it had made her even more aware of what she was going to be missing in life if she married Fabian. Trying to banish these thoughts, she looked in one corner of the canteen behind where the presentation was taking place. She could make out the familiar face of Sam, one of her medical centre colleagues. Sam was with a woman and they were holding hands.

So Sam has a woman in his life! He was a year or two older than Fabian and was quite good-looking in an academic way—and although he didn't press any buttons for Clare, she could imagine that other women might find him attractive. He was a bit of a loner and whenever she was with him, having lunch at the local pub for instance, she was amused to notice how secretive he always was about his private life.

As she was mulling over these thoughts, she caught a glimpse of the woman. Up until that moment she'd kept her head lowered, her face half-hidden by her straight blonde hair. When she lifted her head, Clare recognised her. She'd been introduced to her at the pub one lunchtime. It was Catrina, Brian's girlfriend. Catrina the super-nurse.

What was she doing with Sam? Clare wondered idly. It was a little odd—Brian was away on holiday, presumably on his own, while Catrina was here in the canteen holding hands with Sam. Her curiosity aroused, Clare continued to look at them while she finished her cup of tea. Speculating about someone else was a good way of taking her mind off her own worries.

The table where Sam and Catrina were sitting was

in one of the more secluded areas which probably explained why Sam, without even checking if he was being watched, leaned across the table and kissed Catrina on the lips.

Goodness, thought Clare, that's a turn-up for the books! *Sam and Catrina!*

'I wonder if Brian knows about it?' she muttered quietly to herself.

The next day, she, Fabian and Sam were having their usual lunch in the pub. Clare hadn't mentioned to Fabian what she'd previously seen but she couldn't resist bringing up the subject now that the three of them were together. She was also interested to see how Sam would react—and indeed if there was a perfectly simple explanation.

'I saw you in Maggie's canteen yesterday with Catrina,' she said, not being a person who minced words.

Sam stiffened defensively. 'Did you? I might have been there… Oh, yes, I think I was. I just called in to Maggie's to check on something…to check on a patient of mine who's having dialysis…a patient that Catrina had also been attending to.'

Sam was definitely acting guiltily, reeling off yards of explanations when she hadn't even enquired why he'd been there.

'Was Catrina upset about something?' she asked. 'I noticed you were holding her hand.'

Sam shot a glance at Fabian, then back to Clare before answering. 'What is this? The Spanish Inquisition?'

'Not at all!' said Clare, smiling innocently. 'I was surprised that Catrina wasn't on holiday with Brian, that's all. I thought those two were a really big item.'

'I thought Brian said he was going on holiday with Catrina,' Fabian interjected. 'That's what he told me, anyway.'

Sam was by this time looking decidedly uncomfortable. 'She called it off.'

'The holiday?' asked Fabian.

'The relationship with Brian,' said Sam.

Fabian gave a sharp intake of breath.

'I thought as much,' said Clare. 'You're a sly one, pinching old Brian's woman from under his nose.'

'Hang on, Clare,' said Fabian. 'Just because Catrina isn't on holiday with Brian doesn't mean she's having an affair with Sam! You can sit at a canteen table with someone and *not* be having it off with them, you know!'

'Holding hands? Kissing?' said Clare.

She hadn't intended to upset Sam. She'd just been acting playfully, she thought. In her family this kind of teasing banter was commonplace and part of her everyday life. She was surprised, therefore, when Sam turned on her viciously.

'Just mind your own business, will you?' he snarled, pushing his chair back noisily and striding out of the pub.

'Well,' she said, 'what did I say? What's rattled his cage?'

Fabian stared out across the crowded room. 'I don't know. But I hope everything's all right with Brian. We've been here before with him—when his wife left.'

Clare felt herself go cold. What was it Brian had told her the first time they'd come here for lunch? Something to do with being an alcoholic—and how he'd started drinking when his wife had left him…and how he'd been saved from the demon drink by the wonderful Catrina. Catrina the super-nurse.

'When's he due back at The Hawthorns?' she asked.

'Tomorrow,' said Fabian. 'Let's hope the holiday did him good and he's able to get over the break-up—and the fact that his former girlfriend is now going out with his partner.'

'I wonder if he knows?' said Clare. 'From the way that Sam's been behaving it sounds as if they might be trying to keep that a secret. I'm certainly not going to mention it to him.'

'Nor me,' said Fabian, sighing deeply. He was truly very worried about Brian.

They stayed in the pub a little longer, finishing their lunch. It was the first time they'd been alone together since their return from Florida. They'd slipped back into being 'just friends'—a situation Clare wouldn't have believed possible when they'd gone so far into a relationship. Because Brian's holiday locum was only at The Hawthorns part-time the three regulars had been extra busy during working hours—and Fabian hadn't suggested any socialising. On Clare's part, she'd decided to let things cool down a little before picking up the strands of their earlier friendship. Although Fabian didn't seem to have sunk into the kind of depressive mood that had so shocked and upset her in Florida, he didn't appear to want to patch things up too quickly either. He hadn't even mentioned their earlier quarrel.

She was therefore quite surprised when he said in a low voice, 'By the way, did you get your period when it was due?'

She nearly choked on her tuna sandwich.

'What?'

Her mind was still dwelling on the possibility of Sam

and Catrina having a secret affair and hadn't been expecting the question.

'Your menstrual period,' he said, his voice barely audible, his face tense.

'I heard you the first time,' she said. 'I just couldn't believe my ears. Yes, Dr Drumm, you can relax. I'm not pregnant.'

He breathed deeply, leaning back against his chair.

'Thank God,' he uttered.

The look of total relief on his face disgusted her.

'Well, that's nice to know, isn't it? Nice to know how you feel about me as a prospective wife and mother! I'm sorry the idea of fatherhood revolts you so much—or was it just the idea of *me* being the mother of your child that you find so repellent?' She opened her handbag and fished out her purse. Grabbing some money she slapped it down on the table—at the same time rising from her chair.

'Pay the bill, will you? And I won't be coming here for lunch again. I don't want to sit at the same table as someone like you.'

She left him sitting alone at the table, his face an unreadable mask. Because he'd shown so little emotion, apart from the exclamation of relief when he'd heard that she wasn't pregnant, Clare was also able to remain outwardly cold. She was glad of that—the last thing she wanted was for her volatile nature to let her down and to end up either raising her voice to him or blubbing into her cappuccino.

When she got home that Friday evening there was a message on her answering-machine from a very contrite Sam telling her how sorry he was for being so rude to her at lunchtime and that he hoped she'd forgive him. No further explanation was forthcoming

about whether or not she'd jumped to the wrong conclusion about him and Catrina.

After the weekend, which she spent at her parents'
home, she drove into the car park at The Hawthorns.
A few seconds later, Brian parked his car next to hers
and they walked into the medical centre together.

Clare was wary of putting her foot in it and therefore
kept the conversation on a safe level, enquiring in general terms about his holiday.

'You had a good rest, did you?' she asked, giving
him a bright smile.

'Indeed we did,' he replied.

'Go anywhere nice,' she asked, 'or did you just stay
at home?'

'We went away to Scotland,' he said. 'It's lovely at
this time of year.'

'We?' she queried.

'Catrina and I,' he said, holding open the door of
the medical centre.

As she passed in front of him she noticed a strong
smell of alcohol on his breath.

After morning surgery, Clare sat at her desk, doodling
on a scrap of paper. She was undecided about whether
she should mention her earlier conversation with Brian
to Sam or Fabian.

She was particularly concerned about the fact that
Brian seemed to be drinking again. Under normal circumstances she would have simply spoken to the other
partners about it. But things weren't simple any more—
not since she'd seen Sam kissing Catrina, and certainly
not since Fabian had acted so despicably when he'd
discovered she wasn't pregnant.

However, she felt she had to say something to someone—and speaking to Fabian was probably the easier option.

She knocked on his door and went in. When he saw who it was his face relaxed into a welcoming smile—but only momentarily. In an instant it was as if a shutter had been pulled down in front of his eyes blocking out all hint of personal feeling.

'Hi,' he said formally. 'What can I do for you, Clare?'

She closed the door behind her and went up to him. 'I'm worried about Brian,' she said in a low voice.

'At least he's back,' said Fabian. 'That must be a good sign. It must mean he's not taking the break-up too hard.'

'That's just it,' she said, 'he's acting as if he's in denial. He's pretending that everything's just as it always was. He even told me that Catrina went on holiday with him.'

'Oh, dear,' said Fabian clicking his tongue against the roof of his mouth.

'And another thing,' she continued, 'he's been drinking again.'

At this news Fabian shut his eyes briefly. 'Are you sure?'

'I could smell it on his breath,' she said. 'Unless he's using a new brand of whisky-flavoured toothpaste.'

True to her word, she didn't join them in the Builders' Arms for lunch, choosing instead to walk into town and buy a sandwich and eat it sitting on a bench in the small park.

The Brian-Sam-Catrina business had temporarily taken her mind off her own break-up with Fabian.

Fabian, she mused, might still be under the impression that they were still 'friends' but as far as she was concerned it was definitely all over, even the friendship bit. He was just a medical partner now, that was all. If ever she found herself yearning for the love they'd once shared, she only had to recall the look of relief on his face when she'd told him she wasn't pregnant. She kept analysing that look…it had been one of deliverance almost, with more than a hint of triumph. She shuddered at the memory. It was something she never wanted to experience again as long as she lived.

Later that day, Fabian popped his head round her door. After checking that she was alone he stepped inside.

'I spoke to Brian at lunch,' he said. 'It was more than a little awkward because Sam was also there—but you're right about him being in denial. He talked several times about the holiday and about Catrina being with him. I didn't dare look at Sam for fear he might say something.'

'Do you think he knows? About Sam and Catrina?' Clare asked.

Fabian shook his head. 'Most unlikely, I'd say. I think he's pretending everything is normal in the hope that Catrina will come back to him. If he knew that Sam was involved he wouldn't be attempting to hoodwink us.'

'In that case shouldn't we say something? Don't you think we owe it to Brian to tell him what we know?' ventured Clare.

'Not yet,' said Fabian. 'He's going to find out some time, but maybe it's better if he gets used to being without Catrina before learning that the ''other man'' is one of his partners. That's what happened last time.'

'Last time?'

'Brian's wife ran off with a colleague from The Hawthorns. That's what turned him to drink. He couldn't believe that the two people he'd trusted implicitly had duped him and cheated on him.'

'Oh, no,' said Clare, a great cloud of gloom descending on her and adding even more to the gloominess she was already feeling.

'Still,' said Fabian with a shrug, 'at least he doesn't seem to be drinking again. He ordered his usual soft drink at lunchtime and even made some comment about being teetotal. I think you might have been mistaken about the alcohol on his breath. I didn't notice anything.'

'It's amazing what a handful of peppermints will do,' said Clare cynically.

He made as if to leave, then turned back to face her. 'I'm meeting your brother tonight,' he said.

'Simon? He never said anything to me.'

'He rang me this morning. He's got a special Ferrari that he thinks I might be interested in.'

'And might you?'

'At the right price. You only live once,' he said, 'so you might as well live it to the full.'

'Owning a Ferrari is living life to the full, is it?' She tried hard to keep the bitterness out of her voice but didn't succeed.

'I adore fast cars,' he said.

'Fast cars and yourself—your two most favourite things,' she said, not even pretending to be joking.

'I'm pretty fond of you, you know,' he said a touch regretfully.

'There's not much love left for me, though, is there? It's a pretty crowded relationship with the two of you—

and it's hard to compete with a Ferrari, even if I wanted to.'

'I was going to ask if you wanted to come along for the ride,' he said, 'but I suppose that would be a waste of breath?'

'A complete waste of breath.'

He shrugged and closed the door firmly behind him.

Fabian checked his watch for the umpteenth time, aware that since Florida he was developing some kind of compulsive clock-watching syndrome. It was almost nine—the time in the evening that he'd arranged for Simon to bring the Ferrari to The Hawthorns for a test drive.

'Must stop doing that,' he muttered to himself. He put his hand over his watch to prevent himself checking the time once more. It was as if he needed to fill every second with activity of some kind or another in order not to be left with any spare time—time in which his thoughts would inevitably turn to his terrible predicament.

'Think about something else,' he told himself.

He decided to go and wait outside in the car park for Simon to arrive. First of all he made his way to Brian's room. Brian was working late catching up on paperwork that had built up while he'd been on holiday—he was also on call that evening. Fabian still had a worrying concern about his senior partner because of the strange way he was behaving over Catrina. As he walked to Brian's room he mulled over the various reasons why the man should act as if nothing had changed in his relationship with his girlfriend and came to the conclusion that it was merely Brian's way of coping with the uncontrollable, of blotting out reality—

very much along the lines of Fabian's compulsive clock-watching.

Brian was sitting at his desk with his head in his hands.

'Are you all right?' Fabian asked.

Brian looked up blearily. It was hard to tell whether his eyes were bloodshot through crying or for some other reason.

'Yes, I'm fine,' he replied. His words were slurred.

Alarm bells rang in Fabian's head.

'Have you been drinking?' He walked over to Brian's desk and attempted to pull open the bottom drawer. Brian held the drawer shut with his knee but not before Fabian had heard the telltale sound of clinking bottles coming from within.

'Leave it,' said Brian. 'It's my problem not yours.'

'Of course it's my problem!' said Fabian who, now that he was closer, noticed a very strong smell of alcohol. Whether the smell was coming from Brian's breath or from the desk drawer was not entirely clear— probably a combination of both.

Fabian was appalled. 'You're on call tonight, for God's sake!' He pointed a warning finger at his errant partner. 'You must not, under any circumstances, go out to see a patient. Promise me you won't.'

Brian stared at him defiantly. 'I'm perfectly capable of doing my job. I've only had a couple of tots—just before you came in. That's why you can smell it.'

Fabian banged his fist on the desk making several items jump in the air.

'You're drunk! You wouldn't be in this state after a couple of tots.'

Brian, now red in the face, attempted to stand up

but, in doing so, stumbled and fell to the floor. Fabian helped him back to his chair.

'I'm going to call our emergency on-call service and switch the practice over to it for tonight,' he said in a firm, low voice. 'You're in no fit state to even drive let alone practise medicine.'

'I still think you're overreacting. I just need something to eat and then I'll be fine.' Brian leaned his head in his hands once again in the same way he'd done when Fabian first entered the room. 'It's Catrina,' he said, his words muffled and indistinct.

'I know, mate,' said Fabian gently, patting him on the back. 'I heard about it.'

'I thought she might come back. I couldn't believe she'd leave me—not like that.' He seemed close to tears.

Fabian didn't want to say anything that might make matters worse. He just stood in silence and wondered what his first priority should be—phoning their emergency call line or checking the car park for Simon.

'It's Sam, you know,' said Brian eventually.

'Sam?' Fabian still didn't want to inadvertently say the wrong thing.

'He told me after lunch. He said he'd been feeling guilty about me not knowing about him and Catrina.' Brian looked up, red-eyed. 'My own partner running off with my girlfriend! Can you credit it? Of course he wasn't to know about Jim and my wife, I suppose.'

Jim was Brian's former partner, the man who'd had an affair with Brian's wife.

'What did you say to Sam?' Fabian enquired.

'Not much. I just called in at the off-licence instead and bought some more whisky. It helps to numb you.

It works, actually. I don't feel as angry as perhaps I should, that's for sure.'

'So, it's agreed that you're not on call tonight?'

Brian nodded reluctantly.

Fabian checked his watch again, cursing himself as he did.

'What's the matter?' Brian asked.

'Nothing. I'm expecting someone in a few minutes.'

At that moment the doorbell rang.

'That'll be him,' said Fabian. 'He's taking me out for a test drive in a car I might be buying. I won't be long, but before I leave I'll switch us over to the emergency on-call service. Agreed?'

Brian nodded again, shamefaced.

'And you're not to drive home tonight,' said Fabian. 'When I get back from the test drive I'll give you a lift and you can leave your car here overnight. I'll pick you up again in the morning. All right?'

Brian made a valiant attempt to smile. 'Yes, nanny,' he said, winking one of his bloodshot eyes.

The Ferrari was superb. Fabian had never driven one before. After being shown all the various controls by Simon, he took the wheel and carefully nosed the sexy red convertible out of The Hawthorns' car park.

They drove around for about twenty minutes. Fabian decided almost at once that this was a car he could get along with very nicely, thank you.

'How much are you asking?' he said to Simon.

'Sixty-five K,' came the reply.

'Are you sure?' Fabian had taken the precaution of buying a used-car price guide that afternoon. The price quoted by Simon was quite a bargain..

'Absolutely sure,' replied Simon. 'It may sound a

lot—but for a two-year-old Ferrari Spider, believe me, that's a very good price.'

'I know it is,' said Fabian, biting his tongue. If Simon was prepared to sell the car at such a give-away price, who was he to offer more? 'I'm very tempted to buy it. I'll contact you tomorrow with my answer—but like I said, I'm very tempted.'

He felt happy driving the car. And he might as well use his legacy windfall to buy himself a little happiness…what use was the money for anything else? He saw no future happiness stretching out ahead of him as he had before Florida—before his fateful conversation with his half-brother. Brad's 'There's something I have to tell you' had changed all that…had changed all the plans he'd had for a future life with Clare. So, he might just as well splash out an extravagant amount on a beautiful sports car. He'd contact his bank tomorrow and arrange to pay Simon the money. Why not? What else had he to look forward to?

A short distance from The Hawthorns they were confronted by a car driving on the wrong side of the road and heading straight for them. Instinctively Fabian took evasive action but he wasn't able to avoid a collision. The other car braked—but too late—and ploughed into them on the passenger side.

For a long second after the loud bang of the crash there was an eerie silence. Fabian was badly shaken and bruised but had been saved from greater injury by his seat-belt. Simon's side of the car had taken most of the impact and there was glass and crumpled metal all around him.

'Simon?' said Fabian, unable to see in the half-light whether his passenger was conscious or not. Simon was held upright by his seat-belt but his head was slumped forward.

There was no reply from Simon, not even a groan.

After switching off the ignition, Fabian unfastened his own belt and leaned across to check if Simon was alive. He found a pulse and a minute or so later Simon began to come round, moaning as he did.

'Can you hear me, Simon?' Fabian asked.

'Yes,' came back the tortured reply. 'What happened?'

'Some idiot hit us. Can you breathe OK? Any restriction in your airways?'

'I can breathe, but it hurts,' said Simon. 'I think I've gone blind...I can't see! My God, I can't see!'

In the half-light, Fabian could see that blood was trickling from a head wound and small pieces of glass were glinting in his hair.

'It's blood from a gash. Just keep still for a minute.'

Fabian picked out the glass from around the wound and then took from his pocket a clean handkerchief. Folding it into a pad he placed it on Simon's head in the area of the cut. He moved Simon's hand to the pad, telling him to keep it there to stop the bleeding.

'But don't touch your eyes,' he ordered. 'I think it's only blood in them but you don't want to introduce glass. Keep them closed until I get help. I'm just going to check on the other driver...the idiot who ran into us.'

Fabian got out of the car gingerly and staggered round to the passenger side of the Ferrari—the side of the impact. The other car, a silver BMW, hadn't come off as badly as the smaller sports car with its much lower suspension.

'Oh, no,' he said on recognising not only the car but also its occupant.

Fabian opened the driver's door and Brian, who'd managed to unfasten his seat-belt, virtually fell out onto the road. Fabian caught him before he hit his head on the tarmac. Reaching into the car he turned off the ignition.

'What the hell do you think you're doing? I told you not to drive! I told you to wait until I got back!' stormed Fabian, furious at the stupidity of the man.

Although Brian hadn't hit his head on the road, he nevertheless fell into unconsciousness, fumes of alcohol rising off him like steam.

Retrieving his mobile phone Fabian rang for help.

CHAPTER SEVEN

THE ambulance arrived within minutes.

'Clever of you to have had your accident right out-side the hospital, Dr Drumm,' observed one of the paramedics who recognised Fabian.

They took Brian to Maggie's straight away, but had to wait for special lifting equipment to separate the two cars before they could release Simon.

'He lost consciousness momentarily,' Fabian informed them, 'and there may be glass in his eyes.' The flow of blood from the head wound had been temporarily staunched and Simon had been keeping his eyes firmly shut as instructed.

'We'd better get you checked over as well, Dr Drumm,' said the paramedic who'd first recognised him.

'I'm fine,' he said, 'but I'll come along anyway. I need to contact the relatives, let them know what's happened.'

The main relative he had in mind for Simon was Clare. He wasn't sure in Brian's case who he should phone. As luck would have it, Catrina was on duty at the hospital that evening and he bumped into her on his way out of A and E.

'What are you doing here, Fabian?' she asked. Then, seeing his dishevelled clothes, bloodstained from attending to Simon's cut, she put her hand to her mouth and gave a small gasp. 'You've been in an accident. Are you hurt?'

Fabian felt contempt rising in him for Catrina, contempt for the heartless way she had treated poor Brian. Then he checked himself. Who was he to criticise anyone for the way they behaved? Catrina's actions were none of his business, and she may well have good reasons to justify them—in the same way he could account for his apparently uncaring treatment of Clare.

'I'm not hurt but I'm afraid that Brian may be,' he replied, making a supreme effort to keep his words non-judgemental. 'We were both in a car accident. He lost consciousness.'

The colour drained from Catrina's face. 'Oh, no. Do you mean he's in a coma?'

'No,' said Fabian. 'He came round a few minutes ago. They may decide to do a scan after he's…'

'What? After he's what?' said Catrina when Fabian left the sentence hanging in mid air.

'When he's sobered up.' He felt almost disloyal having to spell it out to Brian's former girlfriend—the woman who'd been the cause of him returning to the bottle.

She looked surprised. 'Brian doesn't drink,' she said.

'He does now,' replied Fabian.

'Will the police get to know…with him being in an accident?'

'I'm afraid so. They turned up at the same time as the ambulance.'

Catrina pondered this for a while. 'What a shame,' she said as if speaking her thoughts out loud. 'What a shame you couldn't just have kept it between the two of you—you know, hushed it up.'

'It isn't just between the two of us,' said Fabian, annoyed at her reaction. 'Someone else was hurt in the crash—and a hugely expensive sports car was wrecked into the bargain.'

Fabian phoned Clare to tell her about Simon. He'd waited until he had a bit of good news to sweeten the bad.

'He's going to be just fine,' he told her. 'There was no damage to his eyes, which was our main worry— fortunately no glass went in. He needed stitches to a head wound—and he'll be kept in for at least twenty-four hours for observation as he lost consciousness briefly. But I don't think he's suffering from concussion.'

'I'll come round straight away,' she said, 'immediately after I've phoned my parents. I hope the police get a blood sample from that stupid idiot Brian. He could have killed the lot of you!'

He confirmed that Brian had given a blood sample, as requested by the police. 'I had the interesting experience of being breathalised at the scene of the crash,' said Fabian. 'It was clear, of course. I'm afraid they'll be throwing the book at Brian once they get the results of his test. He was as drunk as a skunk.'

'Will you still be at the hospital when I get there?' she asked. 'Selfish of me, I know, but I'd really like it if you were there. I'm sure you're desperate to get home for a bath and…'

'Of course I'll be here,' said Fabian. 'I'll wait by the main entrance and take you straight to Simon.'

When Clare saw Fabian, his hair tousled and uncombed, his clothes rumpled and bloodstained, her heart went out to him. She ran to him and hugged him.

'You look terrible!' she said with deep concern.

Her heartfelt reaction made him smile for the first time since the accident.

'You say the nicest things,' he said, putting his arms around her and hugging her back.

'I hope the car was worth it,' she said, fighting back tears. She couldn't quite fathom whether it was the shock of seeing him looking so dishevelled and vulnerable that made her want to cry or the fact that he was holding her tight against him. The way he used to do when he was in love with her.

'Car?'

'The Ferrari. The car that was going to let you live life to the full. Remember?'

With everything that had happened since, he'd put the test drive to the back of his mind.

'Oh, yes,' he said, 'I liked it very much. I was seriously thinking of buying it…but there's not much left of it now.'

Fabian led her in the direction of the ward where they'd put Simon.

'Perhaps Simon can find another Ferrari for you,' she ventured.

'That particular one was a bargain,' said Fabian, 'and probably couldn't be repeated—but right now I'm just feeling very lucky to have survived the crash unscathed.'

As he spoke those words, another shard of ice pierced his heart…and once again Brad's words came back to haunt him. He took her to Simon's ward and stood at the foot of the bed while Clare went up to her brother and kissed him. Their conversation floated over his head—he wasn't really concentrating on what they were saying to each other. He kept rolling one thought over and over in his mind. What if he *had* been killed in the crash? Clare would never have known why he'd treated her the way he had…why he'd appeared to have changed his mind about loving her…about wanting to marry her and have children with her. He'd seen the tortured look in her eyes when she'd come running to him outside the hospital—a look that had said *I still love you even though you've trampled on my heart and tried to kill my love.*

He came to a decision. He had to tell her—he had to explain why he'd been such a swine.

They stayed with Simon for about thirty minutes.

'Now that I've seen you with my own eyes and can report back in great detail to the parents, I'll go and phone them.' Clare leaned across and kissed her brother on the cheek.

Fabian said to her, 'Let's have a coffee from one of the machines—and sit down for a few minutes. I don't feel like driving home straight away.'

'I'll just phone the folks and then, yes, let's have a coffee.' She went over to the ward sister and asked if she could use the phone on her desk. As she was making the call, two police officers walked into the ward.

'We're looking for Simon Westwood,' they said to the desk nurse. 'We've been told he's in this ward.'

Fabian walked over to them. 'Can I help you, Officer? I was also in the car accident. I've been asked by your colleagues to give a statement about it. Is that what you're here about?'

'We need to speak to Mr Westwood, sir,' said the older of the two.

'He's probably asleep at the moment,' said Fabian. 'We've given him a sedative and he was looking very sleepy when we left him a few moments ago. If it's about the accident perhaps I can give you the information you need. I was in the same car as Mr Westwood. In fact, I was the driver.'

'It *is* about the accident, sir. Actually, it's more about the car.' He checked his notebook. 'A red Ferrari F355 Spider two-door convertible.'

Fabian gave a rueful laugh. 'You seem to know as much about it as I do…and I was the one who was planning on buying it!'

'Did you buy it, sir? Did money change hands?'

'No, the crash happened before we got to that stage,' replied Fabian regretfully.

'Just as well it did,' said the younger officer with a smirk, 'or you'd have waved goodbye to your dosh.'

Fabian clenched his fists. 'Why?'

'It was stolen, that's why.'

At that moment, Clare joined Fabian and the two officers.

She smiled at them guilelessly. 'Anything the matter?'

Fifteen minutes later, Clare and Fabian were sitting in a quiet corner of the hospital each clutching a polystyrene cup of black coffee.

'So you're telling me you *knew* Simon was mixed up with drug dealers—and yet you never warned me?' said Fabian in exaggerated disbelief.

'He wasn't really—and even if he was, I didn't think it was anybody else's business,' said Clare defensively.

'I think it *might* have been my business, Clare. You did know that I was seriously considering buying a Ferrari from him for sixty-five thousand pounds!'

'Good grief, as much as that!' she said. 'Sixty-five thousand quid—just for a car? Are you sure there wasn't a house thrown in with it?''

'I know it's a lot of money, but for that particular car it was a bargain price. I should have been a bit suspicious, I now realise, with it being so much below the recommended price—but I thought that as Simon was your brother he was bound to be on the level.'

She gulped her coffee. 'He told me he wasn't involved with the drugs gang any more and I believed him.'

'Well, the police seem to think he still is. That was what they hinted at just now. They've been keeping an eye on him for months, they said.'

Fabian didn't know what had angered him the most, Simon being involved with illicit business deals and trying to sell him a stolen car—or the fact that Clare had had her suspicions about her brother but hadn't thought to warn him before he'd taken the test drive.

They sat in silence drinking their coffee. All kinds of conflicting thoughts were racing around inside Clare's brain. She'd had a terrible few weeks since Florida and her stress levels were almost off the scale. The slightest thing made her want to burst into tears. Tonight—with the shock of learning that Simon was still mixed up in shady dealings and then getting into an unpleasant row with Fabian—she was fighting to keep control of her emotions. She was determined to appear to be strong and assertive in the face of Fabian's criticism.

'*You* didn't warn *me*,' she said going on the offensive.

'When was that?' said Fabian, puzzled.

'When we went to Paris. You didn't tell me about Jason and his girlfriend and child! So don't start getting at me for not telling you that you might be risking your precious money!'

'I was sworn to secrecy,' said Fabian, knowing it was a feeble excuse. He vividly remembered how bad he'd felt at the time for not letting Clare know that her boyfriend had been deceiving her with another woman.

She turned to him, red-eyed. 'Exactly! And *I* was sworn to secrecy about Simon. He assured me he was not involved with drugs—in fact he told me he never had been. It all happened because he'd been selling time-share in Spain and some of the other time-share dealers were into drugs. He's my brother and I believed him. I still do. I'm sure there's a perfectly simple explanation as to why the police think it was a stolen car.'

'I'm sure it will all come out in court,' said Fabian quietly.

'Well, that's all right then, isn't it?' she said through gritted teeth. 'And you didn't lose your flaming money. You've still got the whole of your half-million to spend on lots of things to let you live your life to the full, as you keep saying.'

The sarcasm in her voice stung him. 'I don't give a damn about the money!'

'That's not the impression I got. Ever since you saw the glittering glamour of Florida you've been a changed man. Spend, spend, spend—but don't on any account commit yourself to a meaningful relationship!'

'Clare, it's not like that…*I'm* not like that.' He attempted to put an arm around her but she brushed him away.

'Leave me alone! I hate you! I hate you for what you've done to me. I hate you for making me love you and then…' She couldn't stop the tears from spilling down her cheeks. 'Damn,' she said, angrily wiping them away.

'I have to tell you something,' said Fabian. 'Something very important.'

'You've told me plenty,' she said bitterly. 'Enough for a lifetime.'

She stood up and flung her empty cup in the rubbish bin and strode towards the exit. Fabian followed her even though she ignored him. Outside she walked briskly, almost running, to where she'd parked her car.

'I need to speak to you,' said Fabian, running to catch her up.

'Go away!' she said defiantly, tossing her hair over her shoulders.

She opened the car when she was a few paces from it, pointing her electronic key at the vehicle. The side lights flashed a couple of times to indicate that the central locking was now open. She slid into the driver's seat quickly, but not before Fabian has also moved swiftly and opened the passenger door.

'Get out!' she ordered him furiously. 'Get out of my car!'

Fabian raised his hands in a submissive gesture before placing them palms down on his knees. 'I said I need to talk to you.' His voice was firm but calm.

Clare was not placated. She banged her hands on the steering-wheel in sheer frustration. 'We've talked and talked, Fabian. I don't want to talk to you any more. I'm trying to get you out of my system. Can't you get that into your thick head? I need to learn to live without you…so what good is talking going to do?'

'I have something to tell you about myself,' he said as if he hadn't heard her protestations. 'I might have inherited Huntington's.'

'What?' Clare's mind was not focused on what he was saying…not at first. She was still struggling to get her own emotions under control—at the same time as trying to get Fabian out of her car.

'I said I might have inherited Huntington's,' he repeated slowly, enunciating every syllable. 'Huntington's disease, formerly known as Huntington's chorea. The disease which leads to physical and mental degeneration and for which there is no known cure.'

She turned to face him, bewildered. 'Oh, no...' she said.

'I found out in Florida,' he said. 'That's why things changed between us. That's why I was so concerned that I might have made you pregnant.'

'Oh, no,' she repeated. 'Are you sure? I mean...how do you know?'

It was all too much for her to take in. To learn that the man she loved, the man she'd hoped to marry, might be a victim of one of the most dreaded inherited diseases filled her with horror.

'Brad told me on that last day at his beach house. His father, who was also my father, had been suffering from it for a number of years before he died. It was only when the family realised what his illness was that the full implications struck them. There's a fifty-fifty chance of children inheriting it from a parent.'

'There's a test you can take, isn't there?' said Clare.

'Yes. It only became available in recent years and not everyone wants to take it. At least if you think there's a fifty-fifty chance that you *haven't* got it then that might make you happier than knowing you *definitely* have got the faulty gene—and that from the age of thirty-five upwards you can expect the symptoms to start.'

'What did Brad tell you apart from the fact that his father had it? Have any of the others got it?'

Fabian clasped his hands together. 'His sister Bonnie has had it for ten years. That's why we never got to hear much about her except the odd mention of "poor Bonnie". Della has taken the test and it was negative. That's why she and her husband felt they were able to go ahead and have children of their own. If you're in the clear, if you haven't inherited the faulty gene, then of course you won't develop Huntington's and can't pass it on to your children.'

'What about Brad?' asked Clare. 'They adopted their boys, didn't they? Does that mean he has the faulty gene?' She closed her eyes, adding almost prayerfully, 'God, I hope not.'

'Brad's also in the clear. But he put off having the test until after his father died. For reasons which I understand perfectly, he couldn't bring himself to take the test earlier. To be on the safe side, he and Sylvia decided to adopt children instead of risking the possibility of passing it on.'

Clare remembered Fabian's other half-brother that they'd met in Florida. 'What about Glen?' she asked.

Fabian paused before answering. 'He hasn't taken the test. He doesn't want to know. He'd rather live his life in ignorance, that's what Brad says. And who can blame him? Brad said *he* only took the test because Sylvia pressed him to do so. I've a feeling that now they know the result they might try for a baby of their own.'

They sat for a long time in silence, the artificial light from the car park casting gloomy shadows around them. Other people came and drove their cars away but still Clare and Fabian said nothing. Eventually she reached across and took his hand. It was clenched tightly and slowly as she placed her own hand around his he relaxed and let his fingers intertwine with hers.

'Are *you* going to take the test?' she asked in a small voice.

'No,' he said.

'Oh, Fabian you must!' she said. 'Otherwise you'll spend your life wondering if you needed to be worried about it after all.'

'*Worried* isn't the kind of word I'd use to describe how I feel about it,' he said grimly. 'Terrified is more the kind of word I had in mind. Certainly that was my first reaction. I've calmed down now and become more philosophical.'

'But you *must* have the test,' she reiterated.

He shook his head emphatically. 'I'm a gambler by nature,' he said. 'Out of George Merrick's five children, myself included, only one—Bonnie—has developed Huntington's. Two have taken the test and it proved negative. That leaves me and Glen. Now, if the chances of inheriting it are fifty-fifty, the odds are heavily stacked that one or both of us have the disease. I'd rather live with the hope of thinking I might not have it than live with the certainty of knowing that I had the gene and would eventually develop the ghastly thing.'

Hearing him speak so rationally about himself and knowing the agonies he must have suffered, indeed must still be suffering, made Clare break down. She wept uncontrollably.

Fabian comforted her. 'I wanted to tell you earlier, but I didn't want to burden you with it. That's why I thought it better to pretend that I was a complete pig, a man who didn't want children…knowing that you'd ditch me and go and find someone else.'

'But I love you!' she said between sobs. 'You could have told me—you *should* have told me. It was far worse thinking that you no longer loved me…that you didn't want me to have your baby…'

He cupped her tousled head in his hands. 'My darling, I know how hard it is for you. I know how much you want children. You'll be a most wonderful mother—but I can't give you a baby. I can't risk passing on this defective gene. I love you so much but I want you to find happiness with someone else, someone who can be a father to your children.'

'And what will *you* do?' she said, tears still streaming down her face.

He clasped her to him and rocked her gently, her head on his shoulder.

'Don't you worry about me,' he said with bravado. 'I've got my half-million to indulge myself in a hedonistic lifestyle. I shall live for today and try not to think about tomorrow.'

CHAPTER EIGHT

'IT DOESN'T bother me at all that they're going to be patients here,' said Clare at a practice meeting six months later.

A lot had happened in the months since the day of the accident. The day Fabian had told her his shattering news.

Brian and Simon had recovered from their injuries and had each given statements to the police and subsequently been charged with criminal offences. In Brian's case it had been drunk-driving for which he'd recently appeared in court and received an eighteen-month driving ban. He was now back at work after spending three months 'resting and recuperating'—one month of which he'd spent in a well-known clinic that specialised in patients with alcohol problems.

Simon had been charged with receiving stolen goods. At an earlier court appearance he had pleaded not guilty and his case was listed for trial in three months' time. With his father's help he'd engaged the services of one of the best lawyers in town and was confident of being acquitted.

Clare wished she could be as sure as Simon was about the outcome of the trial but she couldn't stop herself from worrying desperately about it. If he was found guilty her brother stood a very good chance of going to jail. She took small comfort from the fact that Simon was very plausible and could usually smooth-talk his way out of any tricky situation. But he may not come across quite so convincingly in front of a jury, she kept reminding herself.

With her great concern over Simon and the devastating implications of Fabian's family history, it was little wonder that she took the news that Jason, Carolyn and their daughter Brook were now registered as patients at The Hawthorns with barely a shrug.

Fabian had been the one who'd brought up the subject at the weekly partners' meeting. He was relieved that Clare had taken it so well. When Jason had told him that he and Carolyn had recently moved to Kelsale because Brook had managed to get a place at the prestigious Kelsale Hall school—and that he would like to register all three of them at The Hawthorns—Fabian had been sceptical. 'Only if Clare agrees,' he'd told Jason.

'Are you really sure it doesn't bother you?' Fabian asked her at the meeting. 'They'd be officially registered with one of the others, Sam or Brian or even me, but in a practice like The Hawthorns it's quite likely that you may find yourself dealing with one or all of them. I was thinking in particular about Carolyn. You might find you don't want to get involved with someone who—'

'Someone who stole my man?' Clare laughed flatly. 'That's a bit melodramatic, wouldn't you say? For goodness' sake, she knew him years before I did. I assure you that all I now feel for Jason and Carolyn, a lady I've never met, is sheer indifference.'

And she meant it. Jason and his deceptions—which at one time had seemed to be so important to her— were now the least of her concerns.

'OK, so that's settled,' said Brian, calling the meeting to an end. He'd only been back working full-time for two weeks but already in that short time he had regained his position as senior practice partner. He was firmly back on the wagon and coping well with the loss of his girlfriend to Sam. The stress management techniques that he'd learned at the clinic were serving him well—for the moment at least. The loss of his driving licence was a great blow to him personally and an even greater inconvenience at work. But he'd negotiated a deal with a local taxi firm that was not too financially crippling—and he'd brought his mountain bike out of mothballs and was enjoying a healthier lifestyle all round. He didn't even flinch on hearing that Sam and Catrina were planning on getting married in the New Year.

'That's good,' he said when Sam told him over lunch in the Builders' Arms on his second day back. 'I think everyone should try marriage at least once.' In a deliberate ploy to take the attention off himself, he turned to Fabian. 'Perhaps Sam ending his bachelorhood will give you ideas in that direction?' he surmised.

Fabian shot a quick glance at Clare who tactfully pretended not to have heard Brian's remark.

'I've no plans to change my status,' Fabian told Brian and then, without pausing, asked, 'Anyone for coffee?'

'Ms Heston, please, room four.' Clare's voice was relayed into The Hawthorns' waiting area.

Carolyn Heston walked into Clare's room and sat down.

'You're a new patient, I see, Ms Heston,' said Clare, checking the computer screen.

'It's Dr Heston, actually,' said the woman.

Clare looked at her with mild interest. From her

notes, Clare knew the woman was in her thirties but she had the kind of face that was almost expressionless and as smooth as porcelain. *That's the way to ward off wrinkles*, Clare said to herself. *Never let your face light up with a smile, or at least if it does, make sure the smile doesn't reach your eyes.*

Dr Heston's eyes were very much a wrinkle-free zone.

'I'll change it on the computer,' she said. 'I like to have the details correct. Are you a medical doctor or a PhD?'

'Medical,' replied the raven-haired beauty.

Clare tapped in the change of title and turned to face her patient.

'What can I do for you?' she asked.

'I'm Jason's partner,' came the reply. 'I wanted to meet you and to find out if I could be put on your list. I much prefer to have a woman doctor as my GP. Of course, bearing in mind your former relationship with Jason, you may have an objection.'

As she was speaking, Clare's mind was racing to catch up. So this was Jason's girlfriend—and mother of his child! Because she hadn't used her 'Dr' designation—and also because Clare had had no idea what the woman's surname was—she was taken by surprise at finding herself face to face with her. But only temporarily. The woman opposite was, as far as she was concerned, just another patient. All the other stuff about being the woman Jason preferred to live with meant nothing to her anymore. She tried to evoke that day, months ago, when Jason confessed his deception and had told her he was leaving to set up home with the woman who was now sitting across the desk from her. She was relieved that all she now felt was indifference. Total indifference.

'I have no objection to being your GP,' said Clare. 'Is that all you came to see me about?'

'For the time being,' said Carolyn, rising. 'I'm very pleased to meet you, Dr Westwood. We might bump into each other professionally as well. I'm working part-time at St Margaret's, doing a weekly contraception and fertility clinic.'

'Nice to meet you, Dr Heston,' said Clare, adopting the formality of her patient. 'I hope you settle in well at Kelsale and that your daughter likes the school.'

'We like the area very much and Brook adores her new school. But of course Kelsale Hall is a very special place.' She could have added 'and very expensive'. She checked her watch. 'Which reminds me, I must pick her up early today to take her horse-riding. It's Brook's first lesson and she's very excited. Jason has promised her a pony of her own if she does well.'

Carolyn closed the door behind her, leaving Clare to conjure up an image of Jason's small daughter dressed up in jodhpurs and hard hat on the road to her first gymkhana. Clare smiled. No wonder Jason's former girlfriend had decided to get in touch after all these years of independent living and gather him to her side. She'd need all the money she could lay her hands on to pay the fees at Kelsale Hall, not to mention riding lessons and a pony for little Brook. Clare gave a chuckle. Jason must be blind if he couldn't see through that woman and her scheming. Poor Jason…she was almost beginning to feel sorry for him!

A week later, Fabian popped his head round Clare's door and stepped inside.

'I've just been along to Kelsale Hall,' he said. 'One of the teachers had collapsed, suspected heart problem, but it turned out to be heat stroke. While I was there they asked me to look at one of the younger girls who wasn't feeling too good. It was Jason's daughter, Brook.'

'Anything serious?' asked Clare.

Fabian shook his head. 'Flu-like symptoms, sneezing and feverish with a sore throat. I said she should go home and take some junior aspirin. She's a nice little kid.'

'And does she look like Jason?' asked Clare out of curiosity. 'I seem to remember that's why he was convinced that she was his daughter.'

'She does, actually. Let's hope she grows up with more of a sense of responsibility than her father.'

'Sense of responsibility or not, I have a feeling that our Jason has landed himself with a couple of people who have very expensive tastes. Private school fees and ponies don't come cheap...I'm pleased to say.'

They shared the joke of Jason getting his comeuppance and for a few moments it was as it used to be between them. The easy repartee, the effortless humour that would spring up unbidden into their conversations.

'Fabian,' she said with sudden seriousness, 'how are things? I miss you so much.' She felt her bottom lip begin to tremble.

'I'm fine,' he replied deliberately flippant. 'I've got a great blind date lined up for you.'

'What?' The colour drained from her face. What was he on about?

'Charles.' He pronounced the name in the French way. 'He lives in Paris but he's over here on business. He's single and handsome. Not only that, he's stinking rich and a very decent man into the bargain. I've known him for—'

'Fabian!' She couldn't help raising her voice to shout him down. 'I don't want a blind date! I don't want anyone except you—you know that!'

The flippant look left his face. He closed the door and went over to her. He put his arms around her and held her trembling body to his. For a few minutes neither of them spoke.

'I know that,' he said quietly. 'But I'm not the one for you. And I won't let you waste your life on me.'

'I wouldn't be wasting my life,' she said tearfully.

'You must let me be the judge of that,' he replied firmly. 'I'm the one who has the problem, not you.'

'If I can't have you I don't want anyone else. And certainly not a blind date called Charles!'

He held her at arm's length and stared into her eyes. 'Now listen to me. I know that you are someone who wants a husband and family. You need someone who can give you children and love you and take care of you.'

'Don't be so sexist,' she said. 'You're speaking of how things used to be forty years ago. It's different now.'

'Some things never change,' he said softly. 'A woman's yearning for children. a man's need to take care of his family. This isn't just about you. What about me? How do you think I feel not being able to offer you a secure future? Any day I could degenerate into a helpless cripple, physical and mental, a man who wouldn't even recognise who you are. Knowing that, do you think I'm going to risk spoiling your life?'

'Stop it! Stop saying that! What I do with my life is *my* business.'

'Fair enough,' he said letting his arms fall to his side. 'That's exactly how I feel about my life. It's *my* business what I do with it.'

The intercom buzzed on Clare's desk. 'Yes?' she said into the speaker.

'Is Dr Drumm with you, Dr Westwood?' the receptionist asked.

'Yes, I am,' he replied, leaning over the desk.

'I've got Kelsale Hall school on the phone. Apparently that little girl is quite ill and they want you to come and see her again.'

'I thought they'd sent her home. Her mother's a doctor so I wonder why she's not—'

'The mother can't be contacted,' interrupted the receptionist. 'Shall I tell them you're on your way?'

'I'm due to make three other house calls first. Urgent ones. Tell them I'll be along in about an hour.'

Clare spoke. 'I can go to Kelsale Hall. I've finished until afternoon surgery.'

'Thanks, Dr Westwood,' said the receptionist, clicking off the intercom.

'Yes, thanks, Clare,' said Fabian. 'I owe you one.'

'I'm glad it's not the other way round, me owing you, or I might end up having to go on that blind date of yours.' She forced a smile. She didn't want the conversation to end on a sour note. Fabian was right…he was the one with the dreaded disease hanging over him and she decided she mustn't do or say anything to make his life more difficult that it already was.

'Just tell me one thing,' she added. 'Why do you see yourself as a matchmaker? It can't be easy for you, arranging to fix me up with other men.'

He said nothing until he reached the door. His back

remained turned to her so that she couldn't read the expression on his face which was one of pain.

'I just want you to be happy, that's all,' he said quietly, leaving the room without a backward glance.

Clare swept up the long, tree-lined entrance to the impressive school building. The former stately mansion could easily have been mistaken for a grand country house hotel if it hadn't been for the dozens of schoolchildren milling around the place.

She parked as close to the main door as possible and walked in. The school secretary was waiting for her inside the entrance hall, a look of relief crossing her face when Clare announced that she was from The Hawthorns medical centre.

'Follow me, Doctor,' said the anxious-looking woman. 'Brook is lying down in the head's office. She collapsed at lunchtime and we carried her in here.'

'Collapsed?' said Clare. 'You mean she fainted... lost consciousness?'

'Yes, I think so,' said the secretary. 'I wasn't with her at the time but the girls at her table said she did. They said she'd told them she felt dizzy and had a bad pain. The dinner lady, Mrs Thewlis, brought her to Miss Morton's room.'

'Would that be Gail Thewlis?' Clare asked with interest.

'Yes, I think that's her name. She's been working here for about a month. Nice lady, a bit on the quiet side but very good with the girls.'

'I'm glad about that,' said Clare, pleased to learn that Gail was obviously back on her feet after the trauma of Steve's tumour and how it had affected them both. She also took comfort from the way the woman had obviously managed to pull herself back from the brink of depression—a situation that Clare herself had been increasingly having to manage in the months following her break-up with Fabian.

The school secretary opened the door and Clare went into the oak-panelled office.

'Here's Dr Westwood,' announced the secretary.

In one corner of the room a small girl, covered with a blanket, was lying on a leather sofa. A statuesque woman of indeterminate age introduced herself as Joan Morton, the head of Kelsale Hall school.

Clare went over to the young girl who had her face turned away.

'Hello, Brook,' she said quietly.

'She seems to be sleeping at the moment,' said Miss Morton.

On hearing their voices, Brook stirred and turned towards them. Clare noted that the girl's face was completely covered in a violent rash.

'Oh, goodness,' said the Head in alarm, 'that's something new—spots! What do you think it is, Doctor? Could it be infectious?'

'I couldn't say for sure until I examine her but these things often look worse than they really are,' she said, not wishing to give the head cause to panic at the idea of a virulent infection roaring through her school.

Before examining the girl, Clare crouched down beside her and asked a few questions in order to get a better picture of what the cause of the illness might be.

'When did you start to feel unwell, Brook?'

'This morning, at home. But Mummy said I should come to school because she was busy working. I think she thought I was making it up because I don't like algebra.' Brook's reproachful tone of voice hinted at a parent-child clash of wills—with Brook's mother winning on this occasion.

'Dr Drumm came to see you this morning and said he thought you might have flu. Is that right?' Clare asked.

'Yes,' she replied in the same reproachful tone, 'and I've been waiting for Mummy to come and pick me up but she's not come yet.'

'We keep getting the answering-machine at home and her mobile is switched off,' said Miss Morton. 'Actually Brook felt a little better after taking the aspirin and that's why she thought she might like to go to the school cafeteria for lunch with her friends.'

'It's fish and chips today,' confirmed Brook, 'my favourite.'

'Did you eat the fish and chips?' asked Clare, wondering if this could be a clue to the child's illness.

'Only a bit,' she replied. 'I couldn't eat much of it.'

'Have you been sick?' asked Clare.

'No, but I've got a pain.'

'In your stomach?'

'All over.' The child shivered as she spoke. 'I can't stop shaking.'

Clare gave Brook a thorough examination after first taking her temperature which was very high. The rash was virtually all over her body and the child told her it was itchy. After Clare had finished the examination she told Brook to stay lying down for the time being.

'We'll make you better soon, don't worry,' she assured the listless child.

'Is it meningitis?' hissed Miss Morton out of Brook's hearing.

'It's not that kind of rash,' said Clare, 'and her neck isn't stiff. I don't think it is meningitis but at this stage

I can't rule out anything. We need to get her to hospital. I'll phone for an ambulance.'

After she'd made the call she asked about Brook's mother. 'Does anyone know where she might be? Was she going to be picking Brook up from school today?'

The child overheard them. 'She's at work.'

Clare suddenly remembered the conversation she'd had with Carolyn Heston.

'Is she working at St Margaret's today?'

'Yes, I think so,' said Brook. 'At a clinic. Then she was coming to pick me up from school after I'd done my homework.'

'Many of the children stay behind and do their homework here,' explained the head. 'It's convenient for children with working mothers or for those with younger brothers and sisters who find it difficult to sit down in a quiet place to do their homework.'

Clare smiled encouragingly at the sick child. 'Well, Brook, instead of Mummy coming to pick you up from school today you'll be going to see her instead—because we're going to take you to the hospital where your mummy works.'

Carolyn Heston was hurrying along the corridor to the isolation ward where she'd been told her daughter had been taken.

'Just a precaution until they diagnose what's the matter with her,' Clare had said when she'd phoned her to tell her about Brook.

Clare was standing by Brook's bed when her ashen-faced mother came into the curtained-off area.

'She's no worse,' Clare reassured her. 'I'm afraid we're still no nearer finding what's caused the rash and fever. The usual childhood illnesses have been ruled out, as well as food poisoning. It seems more like an extreme allergic reaction—but we can't figure out what it might be that she's allergic to.'

'Have you changed your brand of soap or washing powder recently?' asked a nurse. 'My daughter came up in a horrendous rash all over her arms when I used some of that biological stuff.'

Carolyn shook her head. 'I always buy the hypo-allergenic products…ever since she was a baby I've always used that.'

She went up to her daughter and put a cool hand on her fevered brow.

'Hello, darling. I'm sorry that I didn't believe you this morning—but I really thought you were making it up because of maths.'

'Algebra—and I wasn't making it up,' said Brook self-righteously.

'I've said I'm sorry. It was just that you seemed so well yesterday. All that brushing down you insisted on doing.'

'I like doing it, Mummy. And it's not called brushing down, it's called grooming. That's the right word. Geraldine told me.'

'All right then, grooming.' Carolyn gave her an in-dulgent smile, pleased that the child hadn't lost her fighting spirit even though she appeared to be quite ill.

'They've taken some blood to do tests,' Clare told Carolyn. 'We've asked for the results quickly and the labs are doing them as a priority…' She paused. 'Did you say grooming? What was Brook doing yesterday? Was it horse-riding by any chance?'

'Yes and it was brilliant!' replied Brook before her mother could answer. 'We did trotting for the first time and Geraldine, she's the instructor, said I was a natural.

I was on Chocolate, she's the best pony in the stables, and they let me groom her afterwards.'

As she went on chattering enthusiastically about her riding prowess, Clare and Carolyn stared at each other.

'Are you thinking what I'm thinking?' said Clare.

'Horses!' said Carolyn. 'She could be allergic to horses!'

When Brook's blood culture results came their guess was proved correct. It was good news in that it meant the child had not contracted some terrible disease, but it was going to be a bitter blow when the news was broken to Brook.

The next day, Clare told Fabian about Brook and the diagnosis.

'Such a shame for the kid,' she said. 'She absolutely adores ponies.'

'It is a shame,' agreed Fabian. 'She's very young to have to learn that in life you can't have everything you've set your heart on.'

Because he'd turned his face away Clare didn't know if he was making an allusion to himself—or possibly to her. One thing was looking increasingly certain—neither of them would be able to have what they'd set their hearts on…

Clare set out on her rounds, calling in first to see Brook at the hospital. When she arrived at the children's ward she found Carolyn at her daughter's bedside.

Brook was a changed person from the sick child of the previous day. The antihistamine drug had acted almost instantaneously and she was now sitting up in bed chatting animatedly to her mother and to the other children in the ward.

'How are you feeling?' Clare asked her young patient.

'Very well, thank you,' said Brook chirpily. 'Mummy's taking me home today but I can't go back to school for a little bit longer.'

'That's good news,' said Clare, addressing her remark to both Carolyn and Brook.

'Thank you for what you did yesterday,' said Carolyn. Then, turning her face so that her daughter couldn't read her lips, she added under her breath, 'Don't mention the horses. I've not told her yet.'

Clare nodded conspiratorially. 'And, Brook, you've got a few days off school into the bargain,' she said to the child, thinking that all children would welcome such an outcome. Brook, however, looked glum.

'I wanted to go to school today,' she said. 'We'd got this really funny practical joke we were going to play and I won't be there to see it.'

'You're a mischievous little monkey, even though you look so angelic,' said Clare, laughing.

'She may look like an angel but don't let that fool you,' said her mother.

'So what was this joke?' Clare asked.

'It's going to be so funny.' Brook hugged herself gleefully as she started to describe the schoolgirl prank. 'Me and Cassie and Freya and Tamsin—actually it was all their idea really but they said I could join in because I'm now one of their friends—we got hold of this really horrible rubber glove thing with hairs and warts and everything on it.'

'A rubber glove?' queried Carolyn. 'You mean like a joke hand?'

'I think it was one of those,' confirmed Brook.

'Tamsin's brother had it for a fancy-dress party when he was a weird wolf.'

'A weird wolf? Do you mean a werewolf?' asked Carolyn.

'That's what I said!' Brook gave her mother a withering look.

'What were you going to do with this hand? Scare one of the teachers?' asked Carolyn. 'That's asking for trouble, I'd say. You'll end up doing double homework.'

Brook shook her head impatiently. 'It isn't for a teacher. The others wouldn't want to do that in case we got found out. Anyway,' she continued, 'what we did with the rubber glove was to cut off all the hairy bits to make it look better.'

'More human, do you mean?' said Clare, amused by Brook's enthusiastic telling of the story.

'That's right. Tamsin said it was more real-looking. And then Cassie brought in a tube of red paint and we sploshed it all over it.'

'That sounds a bit messy, not to mention gruesome,' interjected Carolyn.

'That's what Cassie said, "very gruesome".' Brook put on a spooky voice before collapsing into fits of giggles.

'It isn't Hallowe'en, Brook,' reminded her mother. 'Aren't you a little early for that kind of caper?'

'It's nothing to do with Hallowe'en. I told you, Mummy, it's a *practical joke*.' She pronounced the words slowly and carefully as if she'd only recently heard them.

'When are you playing this practical joke?' asked Carolyn, not entirely happy with the idea of her daughter being involved in an episode that might result in her being disciplined.

'At lunchtime today,' she said, putting on a long face. 'I really, really wanted to be there to hear Mrs Thewlis scream!'

'Who?' said Clare in alarm.

'Mrs Thewlis the dinner lady,' said Brook. 'She's very quiet and creeps about the dining room like a ghost. Cassie said it would be fun to make her jump!'

'Oh, no!' said Clare. 'You haven't put that gruesome rubber hand with blood all over it where Gail Thewlis will find it, have you? Brook, please say you haven't.'

'Well of course I haven't. How could I? I was all ill and dizzy yesterday. They're going to do it this morning…put it in the locker where Mrs Thewlis keeps her apron. They're going to hide it in a cardboard box with a tea-towel over it so that—'

'Brook,' said Clare, taking the child by the shoulders and forcing her to look her in the eye, 'is this definitely going to happen today at school?'

'Yes.' The child, noting the horrified look on Clare's face, stopped giggling and became suddenly serious.

'But why?' asked a bemused Carolyn. 'Who is this Mrs Thewlis?'

'She's the dinner lady,' said Brook in a subdued voice.

'Poor woman,' said Carolyn. 'Why pick on her?'

'It was the others who said we should do it…because of the story in the papers.'

Clare's worst fears were confirmed. 'The girls knew about her husband and what he did?'

'Yes,' Brook replied, monosyllabic. Clare's stern voice was making her nervous.

Clare put her head in her hands. 'Oh, no!'

Carolyn was perplexed. 'What are you talking about? What did her husband do?'

'He went berserk and chopped off one of his own fingers—which the police then showed her in a specimen bag. The poor woman passed out and was lucky to keep her sanity. The story was splashed all over the local press—but you woudn't have read it as you've only recently moved to the area.'

Carolyn stared at her daughter. 'Brook, are you telling the truth? Are those girls going to put that bloodied hand where the dinner lady will find it?'

The child was defiantly mute.

'Whatever possessed you to do something as terrible as that?'

'It wasn't my idea,' she replied, her bottom lip trembling.

Clare snatched a glance at her watch. 'There's an outside chance that we can intervene and get the offensive object moved before the woman finds it. I'll phone the school and get them to remove it.'

She walked briskly to the nearest wall-phone—the use of mobiles being banned inside the hospital—and dialled the Kelsale Hall number that Carolyn had given her. It was engaged. She tried three more times with the same result.

'If I drive over there now I might be in time,' she said, picking up her bag and heading for the car park.

When she arrived at the school she ran up the steps and bumped into a group of older girls.

'I'm a doctor,' she told them. 'Please show me the way to the school canteen. In particular I want to see the area where the dinner ladies' lockers are.'

The look on her face told the girls that this woman meant business—and a couple of them led the way.

'Can we go a bit quicker?' asked Clare impatiently.

'We're not supposed to run in the corridors,' said one.

'This is an emergency,' replied Clare.

'Follow me,' said a tall blonde girl of athletic build as she sprinted forward.

As they rounded a corner, the doors to the school canteen came into view. Suddenly, and without warning, a spine-chilling scream was heard.

'Oh, heavens!' said Clare. 'I think we're too late!'

'Sounds like someone's been murdered!' said the athletic girl. She pointed to a room next to the kitchen. 'That's where the locker room you were asking about is. I think that's where the scream came from.'

'I think you could be right,' replied Clare, fearful of opening the door knowing only too well what she'd find behind it. A gibbering Gail Thewlis, she suspected...a woman whose recuperation from her earlier trauma had in all probability been put back several months, if not years. And all because some stupid young girls had decided to play a prank.

Before she could steel herself to open the door, it was opened from within.

A large, red-faced woman stood there holding a gory-looking object.

'Who did this, that's what I'd like to know?' she demanded of the two of them. 'Nearly gave me a heart attack!'

Clare peered into the room. She scanned all four corners as well as the floor. There was no sign of Gail Thewlis.

'What happened to Mrs Thewlis?' she asked the still-furious woman.

'She rang in sick today and the school asked me to

come and cover for her. And if I find the scallywags who've been playing tricks on us I'll wallop them with the soup ladle.'

Great relief swept over Clare. 'Thank heavens!' she exclaimed, breathing out deeply.

'What are you on about?' said the fat lady, dropping the bloody hand back into its shoe box. 'It's not nice, that isn't.'

'I'm just relieved that it wasn't found by your colleague Mrs Thewlis, that's all. It would have been much worse if she'd found it.'

The woman stared at the bloody hand, realisation dawning.

'Oh, blimey...I see what you mean.'

CHAPTER NINE

FABIAN was relaxing at home. He was enjoying that happy feeling of isolation listening to music on headphones. It was how he tended to spend his free time these days—on his own and blotting out reality by injecting mind-numbing music directly into his brain.

The doorbell rang. He went to answer it, not sure for how long it had been buzzing.

'You've taken your time,' said Clare, stepping inside.

'Sorry,' he replied, removing his headphones. 'I was miles away. Must have had it on too loudly.'

'Those things will make you deaf, you know, eventually.' She walked through to the living room.

He followed a few paces behind. 'I'll worry about that when the time comes. *If* the time comes.'

She swirled round. 'What's all this about you leaving The Hawthorns?' She shook a piece of paper at him.

'I've detailed my plans to each of you in the letter,' Fabian replied. He tightened his grip on the headphones. He'd steeled himself for this confrontation with Clare knowing it was inevitable.

She held up the letter and read from it. '"I have decided to move to France and pursue a career as medical adviser to a major pharmaceutical company."' She screwed up the letter into a tight ball and dropped it angrily to the floor. 'Well, thanks for telling me, Dr Drumm!'

'I'm not going for some months,' said Fabian. 'I

needed to give the practice sufficient notice to find a replacement.'

'How very considerate of you.' Her face was white with tension. 'I don't suppose you thought to tell me first, face to face?'

'It wouldn't have made it any easier,' he replied, 'and it might have made it a good deal harder. Certainly for me.'

'I suppose thinking about yourself is all that matters at the moment, is it?' she asked bitterly.

'As a matter of fact, it is,' replied Fabian with very little feeling. A numbness had slowly descended on him in the past few weeks. It was, he believed, nature's way of helping you face the unbearable.

Clare sat down heavily on the sofa, defeated. 'But what about me?'

'We've been over this ground before many times, Clare. You know the score. There's no future for us. *I've* accepted that…and it would help me enormously if I felt that you could also accept it.'

'Well, I can't!' She gripped the arm of the sofa in an effort to stop herself from crying.

Fabian didn't meet her eyes. 'That's why I have to leave,' he said. 'I can't stay here and watch you be so…unaccepting.'

'It's because I love you, that's why!'

He turned away. He'd thought he was beyond feeling anything any more…but the look on her face, the emotion in her voice… It was beginning to get through to him.

'I love you, too, but that's irrelevant,' he said through clenched teeth. 'It's because I love you that I have to leave. You can get on with your life when I'm not around. Meet another man…'

'You mean like your friend Charles?' she said scornfully.

'That was clumsy of me,' he replied. 'But Charles is involved in my move to France. It's his company that have offered me the job. We discussed it when he was over.'

'Does he know about…?' She found it hard to say the words.

'About the Huntington's? No, he doesn't…and neither do Brian or Sam.'

'Are you going to tell them?' she asked in a low voice.

Fabian shook his head. 'No, I'm not. I've not told anyone and I hope you haven't.'

Clare shook her head miserably. 'Of course not.'

'It's bad enough having the disease hanging over me like a life sentence without having other people knowing. They look at you differently if they know. An expression of pity comes over their faces and their voices change. I've seen it happen with people who are terminally ill. Some of their friends put on an exaggerated jollity, others become sombre and grief-stricken as if the funeral was only days away. I'm not going to put up with that.'

'I'm not going to let you do this,' said Clare. 'I'm not going to let you run away from me.'

'You can't stop me. I can be just as stubborn as you when I want to.' He tried to make the remark sound light-hearted.

'I may not be able to stop you leaving,' she said defiantly, 'but I can follow you wherever you go.'

This option hadn't occurred to Fabian. 'You mean follow me to France?'

She jumped up and kicked the ball of paper into the

corner of the room with gusto. 'Why not? We're all
Europeans now. Once I've brushed up on my French,
I'll be through that tunnel like a shot.'

She brushed past him and headed for the front door.
'*Buongiorno!*' she said with bravado.

'That's Italian not French,' said Fabian with a smile.

'So, I'm multilingual!' she said with a flourish.

Clare got into her car and drove in the general direction
of the nearest countryside. She had no idea where she
was going—all she knew was she had to have some
space.

How many more body blows could she receive and
stay sane? Fabian's illness, or the possibility of illness,
was bad enough—but learning that he was leaving the
practice...leaving the country...was totally unexpected. At least if he was around then Clare felt there
was a chance, a good chance, that she would eventually
have been able to persuade him that her love was
strong enough to withstand any misfortune that might
befall them as a couple. 'That's why the marriage service says ''for better, for worse...in sickness and in
health'',' she'd told him months ago. But if he left The
Hawthorns, disappeared over to France, then her whole
life would fall apart—she just knew it would.

She took a turning off the main road and followed
a tree-lined country lane that twisted and turned. It took
all her concentration not to end up putting her car in
the hedge. The road straightened and the trees thinned
out revealing a ridge ahead and open moorland beyond.

Half an hour later and completely and blissfully lost,
she spied an isolated farmhouse. She decided she'd better start finding out where she was if she was ever
going to see her apartment again, and drove up the long

dirt track that led to the farm buildings. A sign on the roadside had said FREE-RANGE EGGS FOR SALE.

She parked her car in the cobbled yard and got out. The fresh country air hit her like a punch, taking her breath away. She breathed in lungfuls and relaxed. It was the perfect antidote to her troubles.

'Perhaps I'll live in the country,' she said to herself, 'like my Uncle Pat.' The idea of an isolated existence miles away from anywhere, like her mother's brother who lived on a farm in Ireland, appealed to her for about three seconds. Then, wrapping her jacket around her for warmth, she went into the farm shop.

She rang the bell on the rough wooden counter and almost immediately a middle-aged woman came through from the back.

'A dozen eggs, please,' said Clare.

As the woman put the eggs in boxes, Clare asked her the name of the hamlet.

'Doesn't really have a name as such,' said the woman, 'just High Moor Farm and a postcode. The nearest town is Kettlewell, over that way.'

She indicated in the general direction of the sacks of potatoes. A tabby cat was curled up asleep on top of one of the sacks. In the distance the sound of a tractor could be heard. Clare sighed deeply. On the surface, life at High Moor Farm seemed idyllic, certainly on a sunny day like today.

'You must be very happy here,' she said to the woman, her words tinged with envy. How she longed for the simple life…a pretty farmhouse, acres of land, a few hens…apple-cheeked children who walked to the village school…a strong, sturdy man-of-the-soil for a husband…

'Happy!' said the woman, a sneer curling her upper

lip. 'You should try scraping a living up here with the miserable way the powers-that-be treat us!'

'Isn't your husband happy being a farmer?' asked Clare, disappointed that her daydream was being dismantled before her eyes.

'He is not!' said the woman, her initial cheery expression transformed into sourness. 'He's away in London right now!'

'Living it up on the town, I'll be bound!' The moment Clare had spoken the words she knew it had been the wrong thing to say.

'That's just typical of you town people,' said the woman after she'd taken Clare's proffered money. 'You think us farmers are all rich and making a fuss about nothing.'

'Well, I...' Clare clutched the eggs to her, thinking maybe she'd angered the woman so much she might snatch them back, deeming her eggs far too good for the likes of a townie.

'He's in London on a protest to the government. Not only that, while he's not here we've had to pay some stupid lad to work the fields.' She indicated in the direction of the tractor noise. 'He's a complete waste of space, that lad, and he can't handle a tractor properly even though he swore blind he could.'

'Oh, dear,' said Clare, edging her way to the door. 'There's always someone worse off than yourself.'

'How do you mean? What do you know about it?'

'I was referring to myself, not you,' she said, hurriedly escaping from the shop before she was tempted to laugh out loud. From the sceptical look on the woman's face it was obvious she thought Clare was having a go at her!

One good thing had come from the encounter, mused

Clare as she dashed over the cobbles—it had forced all thoughts of Fabian to the back of her mind. She was able to think of something else—life on a farm, for instance—as she conjured up the image of the farmers making their protest in London. It would probably be on the television news. She must make a point of watching it to find out what was griping them so much at High Moor Farm.

The sound of the tractor was getting louder, she noticed, as, keeping her head down, she concentrated on avoiding the patches of slurry that were making the cobbles slippery.

Is it like this on Uncle Pat's farm? she found herself wondering. Does the idyllic country farm exist at all—or is it only in the imagination and in childhood memories?

Then, two things happened simultaneously. There was a shout from the direction of the farm shop and a loud, mechanical sound as the tractor spun round into the cobbled yard and thundered towards her.

She was dreaming about her childhood and about Uncle Pat's farm. The farm and the large stone-built farmhouse had originally belonged to Clare's maternal grandparents. Clare's mother was one of six children and all had left the family home to work in the city or to live abroad except the second eldest boy, Patrick always known as Pat.

When they were young, Clare and Simon used to be taken by their mother to stay on the farm for holidays. Clare remembered them as being magical times...particularly so because they were allowed to stay up late with the adults, very much in the Continental fashion. A child would climb onto the knee of an uncle or aunt and listen to the fantastic tales that were being told, or join in the traditional singing…or just fall asleep.

The best times, as far as Clare was concerned, were when they were allowed to go along with the grown-ups to a crossroads dance.

Do they still have them now? she wondered. Maybe they do, in the remotest parts of Ireland. Or have they died out like so many of the good things from the past?

The music was the best! Played by a small band or group made up of an accordion player, a fiddle or two, a whistle or flute and perhaps a brass instrument if someone managed to get hold of one. Sometimes there'd be a singer, a local lad or girl who fancied their chances of making the big time. Or, if no singer turned up, one of Uncle Pat's brothers, usually Gerry, would let himself be persuaded to get up and sing.

The family farm was near a reasonably sized market town. There was always a good turnout at the dances which were held in the open air at a crossroads. In the early evening the people would come down from the farms. Clare and Simon would be carried on the shoulders of various uncles.

'I can walk myself, you know, I'm a big girl now.'

'Ah, sure, don't I know it. But anyhow, save your little legs for dancing,' would say her Uncle Gerry.

Sometimes, as a particular treat, she would find herself being carried on the crossbar of someone's bicycle.

The atmosphere was almost medieval—the only light, as far as she could recall, being provided by the moon and the stars. When the music began you couldn't keep your feet still. It was magical…the music in particular. That's what made it so memorable.

* * *

Fabian was in the middle of morning surgery when the news was broken to him by Brian.

'Clare's had an accident,' he said. 'She's survived but she's in a coma.'

Fabian leapt up, stricken. 'What happened?'

'She was hit by a tractor. That's all I know, really.'

'A tractor?' said Fabian in disbelief. 'What on earth was she doing driving into a tractor? Or what was a tractor doing driving into her?'

'She'd gone into the country, somewhere near Kettlewell,' replied Brian.

'What on earth for?'

'To buy eggs, apparently. According to her mother.'

'Eggs? Why didn't she get them from a supermarket?' Fabian was in a daze. 'Is her car a write-off? This practice must have put a jinx on its partners' cars.'

'She wasn't in her car. She was walking across a farmyard and the tractor driver didn't see her and hit her…gave her a glancing blow and then she was thrown heavily onto the ground, striking her head on the cobblestones and knocking herself out.'

'Where is she?' said Fabian, distraught.

'They took her to Kettlewell General. They're doing a brain scan and other tests. I phoned them up a couple of minutes ago to find out Clare's status.' Brian paused. 'They're reasonably hopeful that she isn't brain-damaged.'

'My God!' Fabian put his head in his hands.

'I'm sorry, mate,' said Brian. 'I know that you two were quite an item at one time even though you've since split up. In fact, I thought marriage was on the cards.'

'I must go to her,' said Fabian, searching for his car keys. Then, realising he still had several patients to see, he clapped his hand to his head. 'Damn. Can't leave yet.'

'I'll see to your patients,' offered Brian. 'We're trying to get an emergency locum to cover for Clare—and The Hawthorns will just have to stumble along as best we can until things get back to normal.'

'Thanks, Brian,' said Fabian with gratitude. He went to his computer to close down the program but stopped mid-action.

'Brian,' he said, 'about my leaving the practice and going to France. Because of all this, I'll be putting my plans on hold.'

'That's good news, anyway,' said Brian, closing the door behind him.

As dawn was beginning to break, Fabian was keeping a vigil by Clare's bedside. He'd been sharing the hours of watching over Clare with her family, mainly her parents. They were at the hospital's special care unit each day and he was there at night…just watching and waiting.

It had been three weeks since the accident. Three weeks that Clare had been in a coma. Three weeks that Fabian had spent there every night—and any daytime hours he could get away—sitting by her side, holding her hand and talking to her.

The neurologist had been optimistic at first. But as the days passed and Clare didn't respond to any stimuli, Fabian knew that her chances of recovery were growing dimmer. But he made himself believe in miracles. Clare was going to come back to him from her dream world…and this time he wasn't going to let her go. He kept telling her that, when they were alone.

'We'll get married,' he'd say softly in her ear. 'We'll

live together and make each other happy.' He'd squeeze her hand. Once, he believed—or had possibly imagined it—she seemed to squeeze him back.

Her mother had brought tapes of Clare's favourite music to play to her.

'Music is the most evocative thing,' said the neurologist. 'It gets right into a person's subconscious and helps to bring them back again. It even works with young children. Our musical memories are laid down from a very early age…some people say even in the womb!'

Fabian was sceptical, and he found the traditional Irish music wasn't really his cup of tea. It was far too emotional, too sentimental. But he put up with it, knowing that Clare's mother had tremendous faith in its healing power. He put another tape on the player and sat holding Clare's hand, letting the soft strains float over him like marshmallow clouds.

At one of the crossroads dances there was a particular singer, a tenor Clare imagined he would have been. 'Fergal is as good as the Count,' they used to say, referring to the renowned Irish singer Count John McCormack.

Fergal had all the girls swooning and six-year-old Clare Westwood was no exception. He had charisma in bucket-loads. For the first time in her little life, Clare was in love, madly in love. 'When I grow up I'm going to marry Fergal,' she told her amused uncles. It was the biggest disappointment of her young life when her mother told her the next day that the charismatic Fergal already had a wife and baby. She'd cried for days.

*   *   *

Fabian had nodded off to sleep. Small wonder, for three weeks he'd been working days and keeping vigil at night.

Something jolted him awake. The music had stopped. Perhaps that was what had wakened him, the clink of the tape ending.

He looked at Clare in the half-light. She was his Sleeping Beauty. For the past three weeks, each time he looked at her that same thought had occurred to him. The accident had left her with barely a mark. The blow to her head had been at the side, near one of her temples—apart from that, her face was untouched. She looked peaceful in repose. Scarily so. He found it quite unnerving seeing someone who was normally so animated and talkative now looking like a marble sculpture.

He leaned over and kissed her cheek as he had done innumerable times since the accident. His lips felt damp, a salty dampness. He switched on the bedside lamp. There was a tear on Clare's cheek. A single tear that had escaped from under her closed eyelids and run down her face.

Elated, Fabian rang the alarm bell.

CHAPTER TEN

THE neurologist said it was a good sign, or at least it could be interpreted as a good sign. It might mean that Clare was responding to something external or some thoughts or dreams that were going on inside her head. If that was the cause of her tears, then it was definitely good news.

'On the other hand, taking a pessimistic view, the teardrops may be purely a physical phenomenon and nothing to do with an emotional or mental response.'

As the neurologist was talking to Fabian, a nurse was standing at the bedside checking the intravenous lines.

'Oh, look!' she said.

Fabian and the neurologist turned round and were just in time to see Clare open her eyes.

'I thought I could see her beginning to stir,' said the nurse, delighted to witness the exciting moment when her patient came out of a coma. It was moments like these, she told herself, that made nursing so rewarding. She would be telling her friends about it when she came off shift.

'Clare!' said Fabian. In that instant he felt happier than he'd ever felt in his entire life. 'Can you see me? Can you hear me?'

'Yes,' came the sleepy reply. 'What happened to Fergal?'

'Fergal? Who the hell's Fergal?' Fabian said, tears of happiness shining brightly in his eyes. 'My name's Fabian, darling. Please tell me you remember who I am.' A note of concern had entered his voice. Please, God, he prayed, don't let her have lost her memory. He squeezed her hand and whispered gently in her ear, 'You know who I am, don't you?'

She looked at him through drowsy lids. 'Of course I do.'

'Say my name,' Fabian urged. 'Just say it out loud.'

'Fabian. Dr Fabian Drumm.' And then she smiled triumphantly before adding, 'But I don't know where I am. I was just dreaming about Ireland and Uncle Pat's farm.'

'And Fergal?'

She smiled again, her eyes still only half-open. 'Yes, Fergal. I was in love with him when I was a little girl.'

'Well, you can forget him,' Fabian said softly, filling up with emotion, 'because I'm in love with you. I'm on my knees at the side of your bed and I'm going to ask you something. Will you marry me, Clare?'

She closed her eyes. Fabian thought she had drifted off to sleep. For a moment he imagined she might have slipped back into her coma. He turned to the neurologist.

'Is she OK?' Fabian asked.

'I'm sure she is,' he reassured. 'She probably didn't hear your proposal. You'll have to ask her another time when she's a little more awake.'

Fabian felt slight pressure on his hand as Clare squeezed it gently.

'Yes,' she said. 'Yes, Fabian, I'll marry you.' Then her hand went limp and she drifted off to sleep.

Fabian put his hand to his mouth and gasped. 'Did you hear that, both of you?'

'We certainly did,' replied the nurse. 'And I'm going to make sure the whole ward hears about it, too! Oh,

Dr Drumm, that is the most romantic thing I've ever heard!' She went rushing off, surreptitiously dabbing at her eyes. She couldn't wait to tell her friends what had happened on her night shift—witnessing a patient coming out of a coma and then a proposal of marriage! It was like something on the telly.

'You wouldn't believe it, Brian,' said Fabian later that day, still on a high, 'she opened her eyes—after three weeks in a coma—and what name does she utter? *Fergal!'*

'Who's Fergal?' asked Brian.

'According to her mother, he was some chap who used to sing at country dances in Ireland when Clare was a little girl. She'd been dreaming about him, never having given him a thought for nearly twenty-five years, she said. It must have been the tapes of Irish music that had got through to her subconscious. And thank heaven they did.'

'Now that Clare's on the mend I hope you're not reverting to your original plan,' said Brian.

Fabian frowned. 'Original plan?'

'Working in France. Leaving The Hawthorns.'

'Oh, that!' Fabian sighed. 'I'm staying. I've had time to do a lot of thinking in the past three weeks and I'm staying put. Particularly now that Clare and I will be getting married.'

Brian's face lit up. 'Splendid!' he said. 'I always thought you two were made for each other. When was all that fixed up?'

'Clare had only been out of the coma a short time when I asked her—and she said yes. It's early days in her recovery and her memory may take some time to get back to normal—so I shall keep on asking her to marry me every time I see her just to make sure she doesn't forget.' Fabian was grinning from ear to ear.

Brian had never seen him looking so happy. He was delighted for him, a delight that was tinged with envy. His wounds were still raw from losing Catrina to Sam—but life went on, and he sincerely hoped that nothing would now stand in the way of Fabian's future happiness with Clare.

'Perhaps you shouldn't encourage her to rush back to work,' said Brian. 'I'm sure Clare would like to have a family soon—she strikes me as very maternal.'

Fabian tried to keep his voice unchanged. 'Plenty of time for that,' he said. 'I think she wants to get back to work as soon as she can.'

'Don't you be too sure,' said Brian. 'Women like Clare can hear the ticking of their biological clock loud and clear! I'll bet you a fiver she's pregnant this time next year!'

Fabian bit his lip. He knew that Clare would never be pregnant with his child—the possible risks of passing on a faulty gene were far too great—but he was never going to make that information public.

'Maybe. Maybe not,' he said to Brian.

Clare was discharged from hospital two weeks later but was told that she mustn't consider going back to work for at least another month.

'That'll give us plenty of time during your recuperation to make arrangements for the wedding,' said Fabian. 'We can be deciding on what kind of wedding we want, big or small. Personally I think we should opt for a small, quiet affair—and the sooner the better.'

'Suits me,' agreed Clare.

What neither of them had taken into account was the

reaction of Clare's parents, Denis and Deirdre Westwood. The exciting news that there was going to be a wedding in the family was an event of major importance to them. If Fabian and Clare thought that they were going to get away with a small, quiet affair, then they were very much mistaken.

'Your father's waited thirty years to walk his only daughter down the aisle and he's going to make sure it's a memorable occasion,' said Clare's mother. 'The first thing we have to decide is where we're going to have the reception. All the hotels get booked up months in advance around here…'

'Ireland,' Clare was surprised to hear herself say. 'I'd like to get married in Ireland. In the little village where you grew up. In the very church where you and Dad were married.'

'Oh, what a lovely idea!' Deirdre's eyes went all misty. 'Whatever made you think of that?'

Clare paused for a second, wondering what exactly *had* made her say it. Her mind wandered back to High Moor Farm and the day of the accident and how she'd suddenly been reminded of Uncle Pat's farm. And then the Irish music…threading its way through the long tunnel that had connected her dream world to conscious reality. She hadn't remembered anything after buying the eggs; she had no recollection of being hit by the tractor or banging her head on the cobblestones. But she did remember the music, and the dreams—vivid dreams that had transported her back to her childhood and holidays on the farm…and the music they used to play at the crossroads dances.

'I'd been thinking about Uncle Pat and the farm,' she said. 'We haven't been over there for years. Do you hear from him often, Mum?'

'From time to time,' said her mother. 'Pat's not a great letter writer but he usually puts in a short note with his birthday and Christmas cards.'

'Is he still a bachelor?' asked Clare.

'Indeed he is,' said her mother, 'but he's keeping company with a widow called Maureen—that's what he wrote on his last card. It's been five or six years since I've seen him. Time just passes so quickly...'

'Do you think he'd like it if we had the wedding over there?'

'Like it? He'd love it!' said Deirdre with utter certainty. 'Pat was always the sociable one, always up for a laugh. We could have the reception in the farmhouse, which is massive.'

'Do you think he'd let us do that?' said Clare beginning to get excited at the idea. 'He might think it's a bit cheeky of us to even suggest it...'

'We're *family*,' said her mother, 'there'd be no problem, I assure you. Guests could stay in nearby hotels or bed and breakfasts—there are millions of those now and all very high standard. And the church would be so lovely, all done up with flowers...and we could pay to have a professional tenor singing "Panis Angelicus".'

'Hey, let's get that famous Italian tenor while we're at it, the really fat one!' said Clare, pretending to be swept off her feet by her mother's soaring imagination. Secretly she was just as thrilled as Deirdre.

'He'd cost too much,' said her mother before realising that Clare was joking.

'Talking of tenors,' said Clare, 'I was just wondering whatever happened to Fergal What's-his-name, that good-looking man who used to sing at the crossroads dances? I was only thinking of him the other day...'

'You mean Fergal Butler? He was a bit flighty, that one. Anyway, he ruined his voice with the cigarettes—he couldn't get the high notes any more. He was a very good plumber, though, from all accounts.'

'Perhaps it's as well we won't be having him singing at the wedding,' said Clare, smiling. 'I don't think Fabian would approve.'

'Why not?'

'Fergal's was the first name I mentioned when I came out of the coma!'

The wedding was arranged to take place in three months' time. Deirdre's organisational skills in the run-up to the big day were something to behold.

'If I'd known you'd got this hard-nosed streak in you I'd have employed you as our conference organiser,' said Clare's father admiringly.

Clare and Deirdre made a flying visit to Ireland. Uncle Pat's farmhouse would make a more-than-suitable venue for the reception, they were relieved and delighted to discover. Pat himself was overcome with joy at the prospect of his niece being married in the village church and holding the reception at his farmhouse. Maureen, Pat's 'lady-friend' as Deirdre insisted on calling her, was a keen and very knowledgeable gardener and had transformed the lawn and flower-beds surrounding the farmhouse into things of exquisite beauty.

The village church was just as Clare remembered it, even though the kindly old parish priest had long since been replaced by a younger, more modern man.

Mrs Westwood had overseen everything from wedding invitations to wedding outfits, consulting Clare whenever she deemed it necessary—but her daughter, still recovering her former strength, had willingly delegated most of the arrangements to her mother.

Three of her mother's brothers lived in Ireland, another in America—and he was hoping to make a trip over to the 'old country' for the wedding. Her only sister, Maeve, lived in England and would be travelling from England, as would her father's relatives. Marie-Paul would be coming from Paris.

Fabian had considered asking Jason to be his best man now that he and Clare appeared to be back on speaking terms, but he thought better of it and asked Simon instead. This gesture towards Clare's wayward brother really touched his wife-to-be which, if Fabian was honest with himself, was the main reason for asking him.

'Simon is a bit low at the moment, waiting for the trial, and it was so nice of you to ask him,' said Clare.

Simon's trial had been adjourned at the prosecution's request and was not due to take place until some weeks after the wedding. In the months since being charged with receiving stolen goods, Simon's personality had undergone a dramatic change. He was now a much more responsible person appearing, genuinely, to have left far behind him his former life and the bad company he had been keeping.

'What a pity it took a criminal charge to make him see the error of his ways,' Clare remarked to Fabian a week before the wedding.

'Just like it took seeing you in a coma to make me see the error of mine,' he replied, a tender expression on his face as he pulled her to him and kissed her. 'Until that moment I believed I was doing the right thing in distancing myself from you. But when I realised that because of the accident it was you who'd distanced yourself from me—and that it might be permanent—I knew we had to be together, to face the future together.'

He cupped her face in his hands and stared at her, his eyes darkly possessive. 'How could I even have *considered* leaving you? My life is worthless without you by my side.' He bent and again kissed her mouth. 'No regrets?' he asked.

'Regrets?' she said huskily.

'About children. About me not being able to give you babies of your own.' He didn't find it easy spelling it out in such plain language but he knew that the ground had to be covered before their marriage. He *had* to know that she was sure about what marriage to him would mean—and what she would be giving up.

She ran a finger over his strong, sensual mouth, feeling it quiver under her touch. 'I've told you before and I'll say it again. I want to marry you because I love you more than I've ever loved anyone. We can adopt children if we feel that's what we'd like to do—but we can discuss that when the time comes.'

'We may have to talk about it sooner than you think,' said Fabian, recalling his earlier conversation with Brian. 'Once they know marriage is on the cards people make comments all the time hinting directly or indirectly about having babies. It was one of the first things that Brian mentioned when I told him we were getting married. ''Women can hear the ticking of their biological clock'', he said before betting me a fiver that you'd be pregnant by next year.'

Clare sighed. 'I know… I get it all the time from my mother. She's desperate to be a granny and I haven't the heart to tell her that it isn't going to happen.' She sounded wistful. 'There are alternatives to adopting, of course. We could consider donor insemination.'

Fabian looked into the far distance. A shaft of pain cut through him.

'No,' he said.

'Why not?'

'If I can't give you babies, I don't want you pregnant with another man's child.' His eyes were dark and brooding.

'But you said you'd agree to adoption,' remarked Clare, bemused. 'That's the same thing…bringing up someone else's children.'

'No, it isn't. Not to my mind. Obviously donor insemination works fine for many couples but it wouldn't do for me, not with all the emotional baggage I'd bring along.'

'Emotional baggage? What are you talking about? I think you're suffering from a case of pre-marital nerves! I thought it was only the bride who was supposed to suffer from that!' she teased.

Fabian tensed. He hated this conversation but knew it had to be voiced.

'I'm talking about my own family history. The fact that my father knew from the moment I was conceived that I wasn't his child. He behaved despicably towards me because he could never accept me as his own. Adopting a child who wasn't genetically connected to either of us would be totally different.' He threw his hands up in despair. 'I'm not explaining myself very well, but because of my own childhood I couldn't accept you giving birth to another man's child. Call me selfish, macho, possessive—I'm probably all of those things—but at least I'm honest about it. There's still time to call off the wedding if you want to.'

'Are you serious?' She looked at him with puzzled surprise.

'Absolutely. You can still change your mind and tell me to go away.'

She saw the pain etched on his face and her heart gave a lurch. She wanted to heal his hurt, to wave a magic wand and wish away all the terrible things that had damaged him in the past. She knew that the two of them were soul-mates destined to love each other—and as far as she was concerned that was all that mattered.

'Fabian, my love, I promise I will never tell you to go away.'

The wedding was lovely, everyone said so. Deirdre had surprised even herself by the way she'd organised everything and everybody in such a short time and to such outstanding effect.

Nearly everyone who had been invited was able to come. Brad and Sylvia were unable to make it because of the children's schooling—'But see you soon in Paris,' wrote Brad.

Maureen, Uncle Pat's lady friend, had done the flowers at the church and also for the reception. Another woman from the village had made the wedding cake and professionally decorated it. 'She does it as a hobby,' Deirdre told Clare. 'She fits it in between her golf and playing bridge.' Big trestle tables had been hired and delivered to the farmhouse. They were covered with long white tablecloths and were groaning with chilled champagne and platters of delicious food prepared by the caterers—a company run by a woman who used to go to the convent school with Deirdre and her sister Maeve.

Uncle Gerry was there with his wife Teresa and two of their three grown-up children.

'This is the little one I used to carry on my shoulders,' he told the assembled gathering after toasting the bride and groom. 'And look at her now, the most beautiful bride I've ever seen.' His wife nudged him. 'With one exception,' he added to a chorus of laughter.

Clare, with her creamy skin and flaming tresses which cascaded over her bare shoulders, looked stunning. In Clare's hair Maureen had woven wild flowers, and her white dress, long, strapless and elegant with touches of embroidery and Irish lace, took everyone's breath away when she took that first step into the church on the arm of her proud father.

At the reception the guests spilled out onto the farmhouse lawn, and the sun continued to shine.

The handsome groom and his beautiful bride mingled among the guests and, as Fabian had predicted, several comments were made about 'starting a family'.

'Just rise above it,' muttered Clare between gritted teeth. 'It's mostly my mother's relatives. They're all obsessed with babies and children, having come from large families themselves.'

Simon made a good speech, keeping the content amusing and the jokes mostly clean.

'He was warned by my mother not to be too risqué because of Auntie Maeve,' Clare whispered to Fabian. 'She was going to be a nun before she changed her mind and got married instead. But she's very pious and easily shocked.'

'Which one is Auntie Maeve?' Fabian asked.

'The one in the shocking pink dress with the plunging neckline,' said Clare. On seeing Fabian's raised eyebrows as he took in the sexily attired older woman, Clare giggled. 'Looks can be deceptive,' she said.

There were lots of speeches. 'It's always like this at an Irish wedding,' said Clare. 'I might get up and make one myself—except I think I've drunk too much champagne to be coherent.'

Uncle Pat stood up and said a few words about how he'd known that Clare would make a good doctor from when she'd been a little girl and had once acted as midwife to one of the farm cats.

'That's an exaggeration,' commented Clare to Fabian. 'All I did was stand around and watch. But it was a defining moment in my life, that's true enough. The miracle of birth.' She saw a certain look in his eye that she'd come to recognise. 'Oops,' she said, 'shouldn't have mentioned that.'

Uncle Joe, who'd come all the way from Chicago, got up and told a few stories about the young Clare that she'd never heard before. 'He's making that up,' she said under her breath. 'I don't even remember having a fishing rod…'

Even Marie-Paul, who'd come to the wedding in the company of her sister Amelie, was moved to rise and propose a toast to the happy couple—in French.

After the speeches and the toasts and the delicious food and the cutting of the cake, the tables were cleared away and the live music began. Uncle Pat had managed to get together a group of musicians that were the closest thing to a crossroads band. There was an accordionist—who was actually Italian, not Irish—a violinist and a brilliant flute player who doubled on the penny whistle…and a couple of singers, a man and a girl who were 'brilliant', Uncle Pat assured Clare. The dancing went on into the early hours.

*   *   *

They spent their honeymoon touring around Ireland staying in luxurious country house hotels. They were away for ten days and Clare was surprised how, in such a short visit, Fabian soaked up a tremendous amount of 'Irishness' even joining in with the folk singing in the pubs.

No other couple could ever be as happy as they were, Clare decided when they returned home to England and to the cottage they'd bought.

Everything went swimmingly until they'd been married three months. Clare was twelve days late with her period. She told Fabian. He exploded with anger.

'How could that happen? How could that possibly happen?' he stormed. The veins on his temples were visibly throbbing and she thought he was going to have a seizure.

'For goodness' sake, Fabian, it doesn't mean I'm pregnant. We've taken precautions and so it's most unlikely. Calm down, man.'

'I'll buy a pregnancy testing kit and then we'll know,' he said, ignoring her urging to be calm.

'You're probably worrying unnecessarily.'

'I'm getting a kit and you're going to do the test.' His eyes were burning. For an instant she became scared of him and what he might do.

'And what if I won't do the test?' she said defiantly.

'You'll do it or—'

'Or what? Or what, Fabian? Just listen to yourself— you sound paranoid!'

Fabian breathed deeply letting his arms hang limply by his side. He knew he'd gone too far…he knew he was over-reacting but he couldn't help himself. If he'd made Clare pregnant he didn't know what was going to happen.

'I suppose an abortion's out of the question if it turns out you are pregnant?' His voice was low and defeated.

'Correct,' she replied sharply. 'Got it in one!' She walked out of the room slamming the door behind her.

The next day her period started, but the shock of believing, however briefly, that she might have been pregnant had a disastrous effect on their marriage—in particular on their sex life which became non-existent.

For the next two months they shared the same house, the same workplace but not the same bed. There was no sex in their marriage but there were plenty of rows.

'I don't know why you don't go and have the blasted genetic test and get the damn thing over with,' snapped Clare one evening after a particularly gruelling day at work. 'Are we going to have a completely sex-free marriage because of the outside risk that I might become pregnant? If you feel so strongly about it why not have a vasectomy?'

The moment she'd said it she regretted it.

'All right,' said Fabian, 'that's what I'll do.'

'No, I didn't mean it. I don't want you to do that— or at least not until you've had the genetic test. If you have the test and it's positive for Huntington's then you could have a vasectomy.'

Fabian was very quiet but deeply angry. 'How can you talk so blithely about having the test and the possibility of it being positive? You know what you could be condemning me to, don't you? I'd be under a death sentence! You're so flippant about it!'

'I'm not being flippant,' replied Clare calmly, 'I'm being realistic. We're talking about our marriage and our love for each other. I don't want to live with you as brother and sister! And I don't want you to have a vasectomy in case it isn't necessary.'

'I'll never know that, will I, because I'm not going to have the genetic test.' Fabian was adamant.

They ate their meal in silence deep in thought. Clare was the first to speak.

'What is worse than being told you are definitely going to be shot in the morning?'

Fabian didn't reply.

Clare answered her own question. 'It's much worse being told you *may* be shot in the morning.'

She didn't even know if he had taken in what she was saying. But she pushed on with her theory.

'At least if you took the test you'd know the result. It's surely much worse for you, and for me, not knowing the result. At least if it turns out to be bad news then we can plan our life around it. As it is, we're living in the worst of all possible worlds.'

Brad and Sylvia's visit to Paris had been arranged for some time—even before Fabian and Clare had fixed their wedding date. Marie-Paul had planned to stay with Amelie in Nice so that Fabian's half-brother and family could have the Paris house to themselves for three weeks. Fabian had also arranged to take a few days' holiday to be in Paris when the family arrived and to help them settle in.

Brad and Sylvia's trip had coincided with Simon's new trial date. Clare had originally said that she would also fly out to Paris with Fabian but she changed her mind.

'I want to be around for Simon,' she said. 'I feel it's important. I want to be able to give him as much support as I can.'

'Fine,' said Fabian.

'Anyway,' said Clare, still feeling bitter after the pregnancy scare and Fabian's over-the-top reaction, 'I don't suppose there'd be enough bedrooms in the Paris house if you're going to insist on us sleeping in separate rooms!'

Fabian said nothing in response to her provocation.

'Did you hear what I said about separate bedrooms?' she persisted. 'This can't go on for ever, you know!'

'I hope Simon's trial goes well,' said Fabian, completely ignoring her remark. 'Will you phone me in Paris and let me know?' He snapped shut the catch on his suitcase. 'I'll give your love to Brad, Sylvia and the boys, shall I?'

'You might as well—I'm not giving it to anyone else at present,' she said, trying to keep her lips from trembling.

Simon's trial began well as far as his case was concerned. One of the main prosecution witnesses didn't turn up. A further adjournment was requested but this was refused. 'The trial will go ahead,' ordered the judge.

'Their witness didn't turn up because he knew he'd been telling a pack of lies,' Simon's solicitor told his parents and sister at the morning break. It was certainly looking as if the solicitor might be right when two other witnesses had their evidence successfully challenged by Simon's barrister during cross-examination.

By the time the jury had retired to consider their verdict, Simon and his family were feeling very hopeful of an acquittal. The 'not guilty' verdict came less than an hour later.

Clare was feeling so relieved and elated that she decided to phone Fabian immediately—outside the court on her mobile.

'Hi,' she said. 'They found him not guilty.'

'That's wonderful news,' said Fabian.

The genuine thrill in his voice moved Clare. 'I'm sorry about the argument the other day,' she said, 'the one about separate rooms. I know you're doing it for the best—and I shouldn't be piling on the pressure. We'll work something out between us—and if you want to have that operation, well...'

She didn't want to say the word 'vasectomy'—it seemed such a drastic step—but if that was what Fabian needed to do for his peace of mind... She was surprised when he, once again, seemed to ignore what she'd been saying.

'Why don't you fly over to Paris tomorrow to celebrate? Then we could fly home together the following day.'

'Is somebody in the room with you?' she asked, wondering if that was why he didn't want to discuss such personal matters over the phone.

'No, I'm on my own—and missing you, darling. I have something to tell you—but not over the phone.'

'Is it to do with what we've been talking about?'

'In a way. Come to Paris tomorrow. Please.'

'All right.'

Clare managed to pick up a cheap last-minute flight and arrived in Paris mid-morning. She phoned Fabian from the airport.

'Instead of taking a taxi to the house, go straight to the Tour Eiffel,' he said. 'I'm going there with Brad, Sylvia and the boys.'

After handing over the correct amount of money plus

an over-generous tip—because she was still feeling ju-
bilant after Simon's acquittal—she walked the short
distance to the entrance of the Eiffel Tower. She
scanned the faces of the people waiting in line but
couldn't see Fabian—or Brad, Sylvia and the boys.

They must have gone up to the top, she mused as
she joined the queue of people waiting to pay.

The lift went up in two stages. At the lower level
she got out and looked for their familiar faces. There
was no sign of them. She took the lift to the top and
stepped out. At first she didn't see Fabian. Then as she
rounded one of the pillars he was there, on his own.

He'd seen her seconds before she saw him and
moved swiftly, pushing through the crowds of sight-
seers to be by her side. He swept her into his arms and
kissed her.

'Where are Brad and the others?' she asked between
kisses.

'They left earlier. I've been waiting up here for you.
I've something to tell you.'

She snuggled into his arms. 'And I love you, too,'
she said, touched by his romantic notion of telling her
he loved her on top of the Eiffel Tower as a way of
making up their quarrel. He'd obviously remembered
how special it was to her and how she'd once imagined
that Jason had been planning on proposing to her high
above Paris. But Fabian didn't respond in the way
she'd imagined. Instead he reached into his pocket and
produced an envelope.

'This is what I wanted to tell you—but not over the
phone. I've had the genetic test done—and these are
the results.' His face gave nothing away.

She closed her eyes and prayed. It was what she'd
urged him to do…and yet, if the news was bad, could

she bear to hear it? When she opened her eyes, relief swept over her. He was grinning widely.

'I'm in the clear,' he said. 'I've not got it!'

Clare felt her legs go weak.

'Steady on,' said Fabian, catching her as she stumbled against him. 'Don't go falling off the Tower now that we've got such good news.'

There were so many questions buzzing around in her head she didn't know where to start.

'When did you find out? How long have you known?' She was finding it hard to take it all in…so convinced had she been that the news Fabian was going to tell her was about a vasectomy.

'This morning,' he replied. 'I'd posted samples to a clinic in Paris for the genetic test.'

Clare touched his face with trembling fingers. 'I'm so glad you did,' she whispered. 'But even if the news had been bad we would have coped with it, I know we would…because we love each other.'

He kissed her again with passion. 'You're right,' he said as he held her to him, tightly, the city of Paris stretching out before them…just as their lives now stretched out before them.

EPILOGUE

THE following year, Fabian and Clare were back in France. This time, instead of Paris, they were staying with Marie-Paul in her newly acquired oak-beamed *auberge* in rural Normandy.

'It's something I've wanted to do for years—own my own small country hotel, serving the best cuisine for miles around,' Fabian's mother told them when she announced that she was putting the Paris house on the market. 'I've found a wonderful chef,' she added, 'so I don't see how I can fail to make a success of it.'

The inn was located in an idyllic, rural setting outside a lively market town. It had eight bedrooms—seven of which were going to be in use on a particular weekend in June. There was a christening to celebrate. Two christenings, in fact—of Fabian and Clare's twin babies, Chloe and Charlie.

Sylvia and Brad had flown over from America to be godparents, bringing with them Mrs Merrick. Brad's mother had, against all expectations, got on famously with Marie-Paul—and also with Clare's parents. Simon and his new girlfriend also joined the party. 'Fingers crossed,' Clare's mother confided, 'that we'll be having another wedding in the family soon. That girl's a wonderful influence on Simon. She's just what he needs.'

Everyone was cooing over the babies who were the centre of attention.

'Do twins run in your family?' Sylvia asked Clare.

'Not that I know of,' Clare replied. 'I was as surprised as anyone when I had my first scan and two little heartbeats were picked up! Perhaps they came from Fabian's family—but Marie-Paul says there were no twins on her side.'

'Oh!' said Sylvia, a big grin spreading across her face. 'I wonder what I've let myself in for.' She patted her tummy.

The eyes of the two women met. 'Are you pregnant?' Clare asked.

Sylvia nodded, still smiling widely. 'Yes. But only just. I did a pregnancy test a few days ago and it was positive. We told the boys and they were thrilled.'

'That is such good news,' Clare said, kissing her on the cheek.

'We've got some more good news,' Sylvia said, 'about Glen.'

'Glen? Oh, yes, I remember,' Clare said. 'Brad's brother. The one who decided against having the genetic test.'

'Not any more,' Sylvia replied. 'He's taken the test and…' she closed her eyes briefly '…it's clear.'

At that moment, Fabian came up to Clare and slipped an arm around her.

'Happy?' he asked

'Mmm,' she said.

'What kind of answer is that?' he said giving her a squeeze.

'It means more than yes. Isn't that right, Sylvia?'

'Mmm,' she replied.

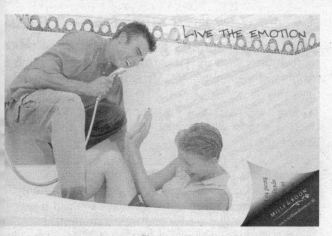

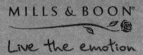

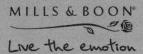

FREE

4 BOOKS
AND A SURPRISE GIFT!

We would like to take this opportunity to thank you for reading this Mills & Boon® book by offering you the chance to take FOUR more specially selected titles from the Medical Romance™ series absolutely FREE! We're also making this offer to introduce you to the benefits of the Reader Service™ —

- ★ FREE home delivery
- ★ FREE monthly Newsletter
- ★ FREE gifts and competitions
- ★ Exclusive Reader Service discount
- ★ Books available before they're in the shops

Accepting these FREE books and gift places you under no obligation to buy; you may cancel at any time, even after receiving your free shipment. Simply complete your details below and return the entire page to the address below. *You don't even need a stamp!*

YES! Please send me 4 free Medical Romance books and a surprise gift. I understand that unless you hear from me, I will receive 6 superb new titles every month for just £2.60 each, postage and packing free. I am under no obligation to purchase any books and may cancel my subscription at any time. The free books and gift will be mine to keep in any case.

M3ZED

Ms/Mrs/Miss/Mr ....Initials ....
BLOCK CAPITALS PLEASE

Surname ....

Address ....

....

....Postcode ....

Send this whole page to:
UK: FREEPOST CN81, Croydon, CR9 3WZ
EIRE: PO Box 4546, Kilcock, County Kildare (stamp required)